For thirteen years now *Perry* **KU-481-182** acknowledged to be the world's top-selling series. Originally published in magazine form in Germany, the series has now appeared in hardback and paperback in the States.

Over five hundred *Perry Rhodan* clubs exist on the Continent and *Perry Rhodan* fan conventions are held annually. The first *Perry Rhodan* film, 'SOS From Outer Space' has now been released in Europe.

The series has sold over *140 million* copies in Europe alone.

Also available in the *Perry Rhodan* series

Clark Darlton

Perry Rhodan 8
The Galactic Riddle

Futura Publications Limited
An Orbit Book

An Orbit Book

First published in Great Britain in 1975
by Futura Publications Limited
49 Poland Street, London W1A 2LG

Copyright © Ace Books 1971
An Ace Book, by arrangement with
Arthur Moewig Verlag

This series was created by Karl-Herbert Scheer and
Walter Ernsting, translated by Wendayne Ackerman and
edited by Donald A Woolheim
ISBN 0 8600 7866 3

Printed in Great Britain by
Richard Clay (The Chaucer Press), Ltd,
Bungay, Suffolk

CONTENTS

1 THE MYSTERIOUS PLANET

THE sun was a tiny speck of light, almost lost in the multitude of stars. It was exactly 27 light-years away.

Sol was replaced now by a mighty glowing ball of incandescence. The blue-white rays of this unbelievable fire-giant scorched the surface of its inner planets. But the star Vega had enough planets to afford such a waste. The life zone of the system reached from the 7th to the 11th planet.

A huge sphere of dull metal moved away from the new sun, beyond the orbit of the 9th planet, approaching the 10th world of Vega.

The movements of the spacesphere revealed unmistakably that it was a mechanism maneuvered by intelligent beings. At first glance, however, one could have mistaken the great globe for an artificial satellite, perpetually revolving around the Vegan sun, but the deliberate changes of course and velocity corrected the first impression. The sphere was the space vehicle of a technically highly developed race.

The ship measured approximately 3,000 feet in diameter and humans were in command in its control center.

Human eyes observed the curved optical screens which were arranged with such expertise that they revealed every bit of surrounding space. As the electronic equipment hummed low, sheets of paper automatically recorded graphs. Slowly a schematic picture was created which held the attention of all present.

"This appears to confirm your assumptions," one of the men said quietly. He was standing slightly apart from the rest and his height automatically drew attention to him. Although outwardly he resembled a human, he came from a far distant system of stars, the center of the declining realm of the Arkonides. "What do you think of it, Perry?"

Perry Rhodan turned around slowly, withdrawing his steady gaze from the graph.

"We can't be sure yet if Lossoshér's information is correct, Khrest, but we'll soon know. However, it is also possible that we are on the wrong track."

Lossoshér, a scientist from the 8th planet of the Vega system, made a hesitant move. He was the only one aboard the spacesphere whose appearance showed that he did not come from Earth. His small stocky figure indicated that his home world was one of far greater gravity. His bulging forehead served to protect his recessed eyes from the strong rays of the sun. His abundant head of hair served especially well to shield him from the high intensity of the Vegan sun's ultra-violet rays.

"I have only noted an astronomic curiosity," said the Ferron as if apologizing. "You asked me about certain things and I merely tried to help you."

"Please don't misunderstand me," Rhodan responded in a conciliatory tone. "As you know, we came to this system because we want to find a planet which is situated in this part of space according to ancient sources. It is supposed to be circling around Vega as its 10th planet."

Rhodan cast a glance at the graphing device and saw that it was now tracing the orbital path of the 39th planet. Vega had 42 planets and there were, therefore, only a few minutes left before finishing the map of the whole solar system. "As far as we can determine now, there is no life on the 10th planet. I will go further: there has never been any life whatsoever on this planet. We are going to try to solve this contradiction."

A man stepped forward from the background, pushing the two physicians Dr. Frank Haggard and Dr. Eric Manoli gently aside. His heavy-set frame had a round, almost flat face with nearly colorless faded-blue eyes. His dull reddish hair stood on end like the bristles of a brush. He ignored the weak protests of the physicians and planted himself in front of Rhodan.

"My dear commander, is it permitted that a little and insignificant assistant may voice an opinion? If so, I should like to state that there is no contradiction at all. The central data bank of the Arkonides mentions the 10th planet of a system which is undoubtedly identical with Vega. Further, the data disclose that living beings who found the secret of cell conservation—and thereby eternal life—had made it their abode Since we have now discovered that no animal life exists on this planet, the only conclusion can be not that a contradiction is involved but, there is an error in the file. We are simply in the wrong constellation. Somewhere between here and Arkon must be another system similar to Vega. I am convinced of that!"

Rhodan smiled enigmatically. He exchanged a quick glance with Khrest, winked at Thora, the beautiful

Arkonide woman, then nodded to Lossoshér. He regarded the sheet beneath the automatic drawing instrument which had just now finished tracing the orbit of the 42nd planet.

"I would like to agree with you, Reg, I really would. But there are a few little matters we have to consider. The Arkonides did not make a mistake 10,000 years ago. Their record is correct. The planet of eternal life did actually exist in the Vega system and did indeed revolve around its sun between the 9th and 10th planets."

"Then what . . ."

"Wait a minute, Reggie!" Rhodan admonished his eager friend. "We'll get to that right away. Since we have made up our minds to discover this world, we came to the Vega system. The Ferrons on the 8th planet could not give us any clues—or maybe they did not want to. Well, they admitted that they had some visitors 10,000 years ago who were traveling through space and who gave them matter-transmitters. They also mentioned that this alien race 'lived longer than the sun.' That was all. And all our guesswork is based on that. Yet those hints together with the details in the Arkonide data bank give us a definite picture. The home of these immortals is situated in the Vega constellation. And now, come to think of it, in the light of two other facts, I should say: their home *was* here."

Khrest nodded his head imperceptibly in the background.

"What do you mean?" growled Bell.

"Upon a renewed examination the file record mentions 43 planets, my friend. You too must have noticed that only 42 bodies are revolving around Vega. There-fore, we have to be in the wrong solar system. Further-more, it is supposed to be the 10th planet. However, we do know that there was never any life there. It doesn't add up, does it? We have a discrepancy here. But Lossoshér helped me with the solution of our problem. He divulged that there is a big gap between the 9th and 10th planets. His information agrees with the picture outlined by the automatic graphing machine."

He took the sheet of paper out of the machine. The hum of the electronic mechanism stopped. The radar telescopes were retracted in their housings; they had scanned all bodies encountered in the constellation, calculated the time of their revolutions, the distance from the sun and recorded all details. The result was an accurate map of the Vega system.

"Will all of you, please, closely look at this map. It will answer at least the question why the right infor-mation can be wrong."

Bell saved himself the trouble of looking at the sketch.

"You don't think that . . . ?"

"That is just what I mean! One planet is missing in the Vega system!"

The interval between the 9th and 10th planets was great enough to imagine another planet between them.

"How can you explain that?" asked Khrest. There was a glint in his reddish albino eyes. As one of the last descendants of a once mighty race whose degeneration had hastened the decline of the glorious empire of the Arkonides, he had placed all his hopes on discovering that civilization which had the secret of eternal life—or at least was said to possess it. The trail was obviously leading them here. And now it ended abruptly in empty space.

"There is only one answer to this," observed Rhodan thoughtfully. "This planet, that once revolved around Vega, left the system unknown ages ago. That means the whole planet, including its inhabitants."

"You've got to be kidding!" Bell protested angrily. The idea was too much for him to swallow even though he had quite a fantastic imagination himself. "You can't remove a whole planet and put it someplace else just like that!"

"You will be amazed, buddy," Rhodan predicted patiently.

Then he pointed to the mapped out constellation.

"This makes it quite clear that we have lost the track. It ends right here in the empty gap between the 9th and 10th planets. The race of the immortals left without a trace. They want to keep their secret, at least that's what it looks like. But in reality they are willing to share it with a race which is their equal. We have evidence of this. The matter-transmitters of the Ferrons, which they neither constructed nor understand, are the beginning of a new trail. The immortals deliberately wanted to arouse the curiosity of a superior intellect, and only people who are capable of fifth-dimensional thought will be able to grasp the mode of operation of the matter-transmitters. That they made the first condition: the secret of eternal life is only for those with the capacity to understand the fifth dimension."

"As if we could do that," mumbled Bell in disgust.

"Our positronic brain can accomplish it for us," retorted Rhodan. "It has already shown us the way to the vault under the Red Palace."

The government building of the Ferrons was located in the metropolis of Thorta, named after the ruler, the Thort. In the cellar was a vault, secured with a time lock, which contained the construction plans of the matter-transmitters. Rhodan had managed to remove these plans from the vault with the help of his Mutant Corps.

"That vault," continued Rhodan, "will lead us to the way. It will probably require a chase through the universe and thousands of years to find the missing planet. Already 10,000 years ago the immortal people decided to leave this system. I am convinced that we will soon find a new clue. The immortals wish to be found some day, but only by the right individuals."

"And that means us?" Khrest expressed doubt with a wan smile.

"If we find them—yes," said Rhodan softly.

The quest for the planet of everlasting life had entered a critical stage. The massive spacesphere had once more flown around the 10th planet of the Vega system and scouted for signs of present or past life. It merely confirmed the original observation—planet number 10 was a lifeless and almost sterile world, which resembled the surface of Mars and exhibited similar conditions.

The spaceship returned to Ferrol and landed on the outskirts of the capital on the airfield of Rhodan's base.

As soon as the huge sphere came to rest on the rocky ground, the protective dome of energy which guarded the base against assaults formed again.

Perry Rhodan recapitulated in a short briefing the results of their efforts up to date.

"It is certain the 10th planet of the Vega system was the home of the immortal race, provided of course that they did not originate from another world and settled down here later. Furthermore it is certain the current planet number 10 was—at their time—number 11 and that the initial planet of eternal life left this area. If we try to contemplate the advanced technology of a civilization which had discovered the secret of constant cell rejuvenation, it no longer strikes us as unbelievable that they had the capability of transporting a whole planet anywhere they chose. We do not know their motives but we may assume that they prepared their globe for a journey through space and turned their back on their own sun. Their goal is a mystery for us but Khrest and I are of the opinion that the vault under the Red Palace will furnish us a clue. We have questioned our positronic brain thoroughly and the information it has supplied indicates clearly that the unknown race did not intend to disappear completely. They simply left this system for the purpose of giving an inquirer the occasion to prove his intelligence and skill. To find the 10th planet in the Vega system is child's play. To follow the road through the five dimensions, that will be our real challenge. We have only just begun the search for the planet of eternal life."

"That's simple enough," Bell piped up triumphantly. "Ras Tschubai has already entered the vault once before, why shouldn't he be able to do it again? He can get the information."

Khrest smiled leniently behind him. Next to him stood Thora, the former commander of the expedition which had crash-landed on the moon. Thora was, for human eyes, a very beautiful woman whose age was impossible to tell. Her attitude toward mankind—which she regarded as primitives—had not changed much. She felt constantly the urge to prove the superiority of the Arkonides to the terrestrial natives. But the confidence of her mind was already shaken. Conflicting emotions possessed her: hate and admiration, repulsion and love, total negation and absolute surrender. She adored and loved Perry Rhodan but she also hated him. Sometimes she even hated herself.

"You have received the same hypno-training as Perry," she said derisively to Bell. "I can't understand how you can make such a thoughtless remark. It shows again the immaturity of the human race . . ."

"We didn't come here to discuss the maturity or immaturity of our races," Rhodan interrupted, winking at Bell and calming him. "Reginald does not know the conclusions of the positronic computer. You should consider that. Maybe it would be better if Khrest gave you the information."

The Arkonide nodded and immediately began to speak.

"Perry has managed to open the time vault for a few seconds. He was helped by some of his mutants, especially by the telekinetic Anne Sloane, the teleporter Ras Tschubai and the seer Sengu. But it was only for an extremely short time. However, it became apparent that whatever that unknown race had deposited in the vault had not been hidden in space but rather in a different time. The African Ras Tschubai was flung thousands of years into the past where he found the box containing the plans for the matter-transmitter. The whole incident did not take longer than 10 seconds. Today we know that the vault is truly a safe made by coordinated cosmic rays which belong to a different time plane. We also know that we can extract all objects from the vault in the present time regardless of where or rather in what time-slot they are conserved. The descriptions found in the cassette were sufficient to supply the positronic brain with the needed clues. Now we have to work out the next step in our program."

Bell caught the expression in the eyes of the physicians Haggard and Manoli. He shrugged his shoulders. It was not his fault that they did not believe in eternal life. It would be all right with him to attain an age of 1,000 or more years.

Rhodan took over again.

"I would like to stress once more how important it is that nobody else learns the astronomical position of the Earth. For this reason our hyper-radio communications with our home base must remain strictly limited. The universe is not entirely empty but is populated by many intelligent races who are observing anyone who is reaching for the stars. Some of them are hostile hordes as we have experienced before. Others even have space-warp sensors to detect any disturbance of the space structure. From a distance as much as 1,000 light-years away they are able to register the hyperjump of our ship *Stardust*. This is the reason we will not return now to Terra as promised. A short radio message is all we can risk. We are going to bring the contents of the vault into the present time and study it at leisure."

"Are there any other articles beside the box in the vault?" inquired Dr. Haggard.

Rhodan nodded.

"I expect so but they will be in different time eras. The new formula will bring them all simultaneously into the present time. We have to reconstruct the conditions that existed when the vault was built."

"They got a real smart hiding place, I have to admit," Bell commented. "I wonder what we'll find there. I hope it will be the formula for immortality."

"That's possible but not very probable. More likely, these immortals will make higher demands of those who wish to become their heirs."

"How can you inherit from people who never die?" Bell posed a logical question.

"Let me put it differently so that your legal mind won't object," replied Rhodan. "The unknown race will make the highest demands of those with whom they are willing to share their secret."

"But it will be a long way to find them," Khrest said slowly. "Much farther than to Arkon."

Rhodan glanced briefly at him.

"I would like to talk privately to you about this—and to Thora if she cares to attend."

The commander of the Arkonides nodded her head.

"I most certainly would, and you'd better have some convincing arguments."

Twenty-seven light-years away the Earth circled unchangingly around its sun. During the last few years, however, the political and national organization of mankind had undergone considerable changes. The expedition of the Arkonides, which had had to make an emergency landing on the moon, had placed such powerful technological advances in the hands of Rhodan, Bell and Manoli that they were in a position to prevent the outbreak of atomic war and to unify the people on Earth. The three power blocs—the West, the East and the Asiatic Federation—still remained, but Rhodan was able to keep the peace with his own organization, the New Power.

His first base in the Central Gobi desert had been enlarged with vast installations. Galacto-City sprang up, the most modern metropolis of the world with fabulous skyscrapers and fantastic skyways.

During the absence of Perry Rhodan he was represented by Col. Freyt, with whom he had established a close relationship. They resembled each other so much, even in their looks, that one could almost take them for brothers.

Freyt was 37 years old; tall and lean, with strong lines around his mouth and a constant look of amusement in his eyes. When he did not act as Rhodan's representative, he held the position of commander of the space fighter force.

Everything was running smoothly. The new erected industrial plants were already manufacturing goods according to plan. The world was becoming economically dependent on Rhodan.

This fortified base had a quasi-cosmic appearance.

It was protected by a continually activated screen of energy, providing absolute security. Not even the most destructive atom bomb could penetrate this screen. Earlier bombardments with atom bombs by hostile forces had repeatedly given proof of this.

Of course, today there was no necessity for keeping up the protective screen, but Freyt complied, as always, with Rhodan's explicit orders. He knew that his chief's precautions were aimed not at humans but at attackers from outer space who might locate and assault the Earth.

The day was coming to an end. Freyt looked up at the darkening sky. It had been weeks since he received any news from Rhodan. What had happened in the Vega system? Had they been able to repulse the attacks by the Topides, the cruel giant lizards? Were the invaded Ferrons saved? Did they find the planet of eternal life?

Questions, questions, but no answers.

Freyt sighed. Rhodan would be satisfied on his return. Terra stood united behind him and his efforts to build up the might of mankind. The first serious steps for a planned world government were already to be seen.

A man in uniform left the next building. Freyt turned slowly around and immediately recognized him. It was Peter Kosnow, the Russian liaison officer with the Eastern bloc. His short blond hair was tinged red and shining in the sunset. When he saw Freyt he changed his direction and walked toward the commander. He greeted him cordially and said:

"If I were in your place, I would not admire the

sunset but go to the hyper-radio center."

Freyt was jolted and asked:

"News from Rhodan? You're not putting me on?"

"I'm not playing games," Kosnow said quietly. "The message just came through. It is being repeated now and if you hurry you can listen to the third re-run."

"Is everything O.K.?" Freyt called, already on his way.

"What else?" laughed the Russian and sauntered off in the opposite direction.

Freyt raced across the street and up the steps to the entrance. Then he took the elevator which carried him up to the receiving center in the dome.

The recording instruments were taking down the message. The radioman on duty looked up quickly and turned back to his equipment. He was just in time for the beginning of the third repetition of the message from far distant space. The hyperwaves did not require any time to travel from their origin 27 light-years away; they reached Earth the same second Perry Rhodan sent his dispatch through the powerful transmitter aboard the *Stardust*.

"THIS IS PERRY RHODAN, *STARDUST*, CALLING COL. FREYT, GALACTO-CITY. TO-PIDES FORCED OUT OF VEGA SYSTEM. THE FERRONS ARE FREE AGAIN. A TRADE TREATY BETWEEN BOTH OUR WORLDS IS BEING DRAWN UP. MANUFACTURING PLANTS B7A AND 42C TO BE PREPARED FOR PRODUCTION OF EXPORTS. POSITION OF OUR PLANET MUST REMAIN SECRET. NO EXCEPTION FOR FERRONS. *STARDUST* WILL

REMAIN IN VEGA SYSTEM UNTIL FURTHER NOTICE. OTHER MESSAGES WILL ONLY BE REMITTED WHEN ABSOLUTELY NECESSARY. HYPER-RADIO TRANSMITTERS ARE NOT TO BE USED BECAUSE OF DANGER OF DETECTION. THAT IS ALL. THE CREW OF THE *STARDUST* SENDS GREETINGS TO ALL MEMBERS OF THE NEW POWER. GOOD LUCK! RHODAN."

The buzz of the equipment stopped. The communication was terminated.

"Were the first two messages identical?" asked Freyt.

"Exactly the same, sir," replied the radio technician. "You will get the written text."

"Thank you."

Col. Freyt turned slowly around and left the radio station.

A treaty with the Ferrons, he thought. Rhodan had thus achieved one of his goals: peaceful trade relations with an alien race. The first trading post outside the solar system of the Earth had been established. But more than that: the delaying of the return of the *Stardust* was a hint that still other missions were awaiting them.

Could it have anything to do with the mysterious planet about which Bell had been babbling on his last visit?

However that might be, Freyt had received his orders.

The sun was down and Freyt began to feel cold. The fans of the air-conditioning blew the cold evening air throughout the dome of energy. He was not quite so isolated from the outside world anymore.

"We have begun a new era in our history," Freyt was talking to himself as he walked toward his nearby bungalow, "but the people don't know it yet."

2 WHO GOES THERE?

THE Ferronian scientist did not hide his doubts from Rhodan.

He had asked for a conference and since Rhodan liked the old man, he had agreed to it. However, this conference had to wait until after his meeting with Khrest and Thora, which was to be private.

The former commander of the Arkonide research expedition was summarizing her position:

"Our point of view is not incompatible with yours, Perry. You want to use our Arkonide battleship *Stardust* to expand the influence of Terra, whereas we want to return to our home, Arkon. We both wish to use the *Stardust* and the positronic brain to find the planet of eternal life. We must try to reach these three goals in such a manner that nobody will have to suffer any disadvantage. Therefore, we have to establish priorities."

Khrest interrupted in a serious tone.

"You are quite right, Thora. I am glad to see that you realize it. Before we make any other decision, we can agree on one point. First of all we will endeavor to find the planet of everlasting life. All other actions will follow from whatever eventuates as a consequence."

"I can only concur with your suggestion." Rhodan was pleased. "Once this is accomplished, I will have no more objections to flying to Arkon and revealing the whereabouts of the Earth to your nation."

Thora stretched both arms toward Perry Rhodan.

"We will make a pact, Perry. We will proceed in the following order: search for the planet of eternal life first; then to Arkon; and finally to Terra. Agreed?"

Rhodan grasped her hands.

"I will go along with that, Thora and Khrest, but I would like to make one minor condition in our pact, if you don't mind."

"What condition?" Thora asked suspiciously.

"Nothing bad," Rhodan grinned indulgently. "Simply that the Arkonides shall not learn the space coordinates of Earth until I give my permission. The nations on Terra are not disposed to become a colony of a decaying stellar empire. You will have to admit that your race is already degenerated, however difficult such self-realization is for you. We would like to cooperate with you in preserving your empire but we don't want to create any new conflicts. Now . . ."

"I accept your condition," interjected Khrest.

Both men looked at Thora. She hesitated but then nodded.

"Alright. I am convinced that the Council of Science of my government will understand your fears. Now that we have cleared up the situation, we can proceed in our attempt to reach our mutual goals. The sooner we find the mysterious planet, the sooner we can see Arkon, our home, again."

"Thank you very much for your confidence. As soon as I have finished talking to Lossoshér, we will go to work."

"What does the Ferron want from you?" asked Khrest.

24

"I don't know. He wants to talk to me. It may be important: who knows?"

Rhodan left the two Arkonides alone and went to another room where Lossoshér was already waiting impatiently. The Ferron remained seated as Rhodan entered.

"I should have thought of it earlier," he began without introduction, "but the possibility did not occur to me until now."

"What possibility?"

"That our stellar system might still have our 43 original planets."

Rhodan was startled and did not answer. He failed to understand Lossoshér. The Ferron noted it without showing his quiet satisfaction and continued.

"You stated your opinion that the mysterious strangers who visited Ferrol 10,000 years ago and brought the transmitters were able to move their planet at will. Automatically we all assumed that if it is possible to accomplish such a feat, they must have left our constellation. I believe that this is not necessarily the right conclusion. It would not be impossible that they remained here, but in some other place."

Rhodan sat down and asked with raised eyebrows:

"And where could that be?"

Lossoshér smiled.

"Now you are asking too much. I don't know where. It is only a possibility which I am pointing out to you. Maybe on one of the big moons which circle our larger planets. Maybe they pushed an uninhabited planet out of this system and took its place. Anyone looking for them would instinctively follow the departed planet, exactly as you are planning to do."

"Your argument is quite attractive," Rhodan admitted cautiously, "but it is pure theory. Why should these technically gifted beings go to so much trouble to make a fool of anyone? One can safely assume that they had highly effective weapons to keep all intruders away. I am convinced that they are playing this game of hide and seek mainly for fun but not entirely without serious motivations. The point is that we are indeed supposed to find them and that is where we have to begin. They have left clues for us and the track is leading out of this system.

"At least permit me to search for this planet within our gigantic Vegan system. In case I discover something, I will let you know right away."

Rhodan gave the matter some thought. Lossoshér's theory could not be dismissed out of hand—it merely lacked probability. To refuse him his wish would not only be unfair but could arouse some suspicion. The Ferrons had their own space fleet and could handle the undertaking by themselves. If the planet of eternal life really turned out to be somewhere around here . . .

"I won't stand in your way," Rhodan gave his assent. "I'll put one of my space fighters at your disposal. The cabin is very small but two people can squeeze in if we remove some non-essential equipment. I'll order Deringhouse to make a fighter ship and a pilot available for you. You will have to keep in touch with us constantly via radio."

The old Ferron rose. His small figure made him appear younger.

"I am much obliged, Rhodan. My success will be

your success."

Rhodan followed him pensively with his eyes.

And finally a third meeting took place.

Reginald Bell had assembled the Mutant Corps for a briefing. The time of the meeting was set in the early afternoon hours of the long Ferrol day. Perry Rhodan did not take part but had given Bell all necessary instructions.

The mutants arrived one after the other. The radioactive fall-out of many atomic bombs had caused severe hereditary damage to the current generation. However, not all of the effects were negative. Heretofore unrecognized potentials of mankind were awakened and became activated. Rhodan had realized his chance in time, located the best mutants and engaged them to work for him.

More than once Rhodan's power had been saved and protected by these mutants.

As usual, Bell flinched as the Japanese teleporter Tako Kakuta materialized out of thin air and almost stepped on his toes.

"I only hope that someday you'll make a mistake and wind up in a blast furnace," he growled angrily because he always fell for the same gag. Then he added in his most official manner:

"Kakuta, if you dare once more to scare your superior officer I'll see to it that you get three days behind bars."

"I'll be delighted." The Japanese grinned and winked at his colleague Ras Tschubai who was just entering the room like a normal human being. "But you will have to see to it that my cell is surrounded by a five-dimensional energy field and a time lock so you'll be sure I won't break out."

Bell did not reply. He knew how senseless it would be. To get over his irritation he turned to Anne Sloane and little nine-year-old Betty Toufry. Anne and the little girl were both outstanding telekinetic wonders. By strength of their will alone they were able to move physical matter across great distances. Betty was, in addition, a telepath and worked mostly together with the other telepath, John Marshall.

There was a total of 15 mutants in the gathering.

Bell pulled a piece of paper out of this pocket, tried for two minutes to decipher his own handwriting and put it back in his pocket hoping he would not forget anything.

"Friends," he began, jumping with surprising agility on a table from which he could overlook his audience, "Perry Rhodan requests your cooperation. I don't have time to make a long speech. You all know—at least from hearsay—about the five-dimensional vault underneath the Red Palace. Ras Tschubai gained admittance to the vault but he made an involuntary trip through time, which took him back to the beginning of the universe.

"Now we will again go into the vault but without the risk of traveling into the past or the future. The positronic brain has evaluated all the latest information and selected its instructions. By utilizing a new formula, the Arkonide energy generator will form a new network of rays which will neutralize the effect of the cosmic rays which are the substance of the vault. Thus all objects inside the time vault—even though in a different era—will be returned to the present time. Then all we need do is simply remove them from the vault.

"You are not programmed for immediate action but you are required to stand by during the experiment so that you can execute without delay any operation requested of you.

"That will be all. Wait in your quarters for the alert. We will proceed via transmitter to Thorta and go on to the vault from there. Thank you."

Bell jumped from the table and left the room.

Sgt. Groll was not very happy about his assignment. When Commander Deringhouse summoned him he anticipated with some excitement a special mission. But his hopes were soon disappointed. Instead of going on a reconnaissance flight with his pals, he had to check all Vegan planets and their moons with this old Ferron.

Like a good soldier he complied with resignation. Assisted by the technical personnel, he pulled out the weapons from their mountings in his pursuit ship to provide room for the scientist in the narrow cabin. The radio equipment was removed as well. Groll received in its place a handy little radio transmitter which was adequate for any emergency within the Vegan system. The contour couch was ripped out and replaced by another seat.

Soon Lossoshér joined him with his notes and papers under his arm. After they had climbed into the small cockpit, Lossoshér gave the signal to start. Thanks to quick hypno-training he spoke passable English although he had no idea in which part of the universe this language was used. In any case he was able to communicate with his pilot.

"The inner planets can be disregarded since their climate is too unhealthy but," he added quickly, "who knows what is healthy or unhealthy for immortals? However, the history records indicate that their habitat was cool. The 12th planet has three fairly big moons and we can start our investigation there."

Sgt. Groll nodded.

"Alright then, let's go!"

And the sleek machine glided like a silvery drop into the ocean of waiting stars.

Thora changed her mind at the last minute. Now she no longer wanted to enter the vault. This left only Rhodan, Bell, Khrest, and the mutants to step into the big matter-transmitter on their base.

The thing looked like a huge wire cage. Generators furnished the considerable energy which was consumed in the dematerialized transport through hyperspace. The requirements were more obvious than the explanation for the method. They knew the power needed in operating a matter-transmitter—even though the operating principle was a mystery to them.

The gate closed.

The gate closed, Rhodan adjusted the coordinates and activated the machine. Nothing whatsoever seemed to happen. This was according to plan, for none of the usual pain could be felt while dematerializing over short distances.

The gate opened again. They had arrived in Thorta,

the capital of Ferrol. The Thort's bodyguards were waiting for them, and accompanied them with all due reverence as far as the basement of the palace. Then they left them to their fate for none of the Ferrons was in the least interested to risk their lives in an encounter with the evil spirits known to haunt the place.

Ras Tschubai scouted out the terrain by teleporting himself to various spots. John Marshall, the telepath, intercepted Tschubai's thought impulses during his jumps and passed on these thoughts to Perry Rhodan. This way Rhodan was fully informed as to what was lying ahead of him.

The generator had already been brought down to the vaulted room the previous day. It had been placed near the entrance of the hall in whose center the mysterious crypt was known to be.

There it was—invisible to human eyes, yet impenetrable for any matter. This crypt was a bell of pure energy, which had been set up thousands of years ago by an unknown race to house and conceal in it many incomprehensible secrets. The crypt was formed by the rays of distant radio stars. Somewhere deep in space a mysterious installation must be hidden which converted these rays into one beam and directed it to the ceiling of the underground vault in the palace. There the beam spread out to form an invisible cone-shaped structure of pure energy. Anne Sloane, the telekinetic, had once succeeded in deflecting these rays for a few seconds. The crypt opened and Ras Tschubai jumped inside. But this procedure had not permitted a thorough exploration of the crypt's contents. Therefore Rhodan had been pleased to obtain a formula from the positronic brain that would achieve the neutralization of the beamed rays of the radio stars. This effect was based on the principle of polarization, as Khrest had explained. There was no time limit on how long this polarization could be applied. At the same time the time barrier would be lifted according to the information supplied by the positronic automation. This fact was of the utmost importance for Perry Rhodan and his men, for what good would it do them to enter the crypt if the objects hidden inside were not present at this time but thousands or even millions of years in the past or the future?

Rhodan distributed the mutants around the crypt so as to be available when needed, ready to jump inside. Then he bent over the generator to check for the proper adjustment. Satisfied, he straightened up again.

"Khrest, Bell and I will be the first to go inside. Only Miss Sloane and John Marshall will join us immediately while the rest of the mutants will hold themselves ready. We don't know yet what special qualifications will be needed, but in case . . ."

Everyone understood what he meant to say.

". . . we should encounter some obstacle, the mutant whose special talents will best qualify him to remove this obstacle will have to join and help us." This was what Rhodan had intended to express.

Rhodan hesitated slightly. Then he bent once more over the generator and pushed a button. There was a clicking sound, followed by a soft constant hum. Now the atomic battery inside the generator provided the energy needed to produce the polarizing ray beam.

All were waiting with baited breath. Were the positronic brain's calculations actually correct? Had the message inscribed on the golden box, rescued earlier from inside the vault, been properly decoded? A tiny mistake was all that was needed to . . .

The subterranean hall with its rough-hewn stone walls was apparently empty. Nothing obstructed their view of the opposite side. However Rhodan knew that this was nothing but an optical illusion: light rays were skilfully deflected and bent to create the impression of an empty space, while in reality energy beams had formed a crypt, invisible to the viewer, an impenetrable barrier to solid matter, light rays and all other kinds of waves.

Rhodan's thoughts were preoccupied with these technical details when his eyes suddenly perceived the first change. The air in the middle of the room seemed to glimmer. The objects behind, the opposite wall, became hazy. The stones appeared to move and change their form. All of a sudden they totally disappeared. The deflection of the light rays had been canceled.

But there were even more astonishing things happening.

Bell remained motionless as suddenly mysterious objects materialized out of the void, at first in indistinct outlines that soon took on more definite shape. The clearer and more tangible they became, the weaker grew the glimmering of the air. The barrier formed by the cosmic rays gradually dissolved. Finally it vanished entirely.

And simultaneously all the objects the energy vault was supposed to protect from the outside world, returned to the present time. They materialized from the past and from the future, lost all properties of the fourth and the fifth-dimension normal time and time-shift, and thus became not only visible but also tangible and palpable. They adjusted to the current time stream, which rendered them concrete and gave them substance. They became reality.

"That is fantastic!" exclaimed Bell. "Absolutely fantastic!"

"But it is real at the same time," Rhodan replied in a whisper. "The best method to make something safe and unassailable is when you send it into the farthest future. There it will wait until we have caught up with it in time. In the past, however . . ."

". . . it would be lost forever," remarked Khrest, "unless you can retrieve it from there, best by returning into the past era in person."

"You mean to say that time travel is not mere theory, no crazy notion?" Rhodan inquired.

"Time travel is the basis of the fifth dimension, the same as space is that of the third dimension. But listen, Perry, don't press me on that point. Just let things develop at their own speed; whenever you encounter such a situation, beware of underestimating it. If time travel were so simple, the Arkonides would have long since undertaken the necessary steps to prevent the events that led to the decay of our star empire."

That sounded logical enough and Perry no longer insisted on more details. Next to him, Bell was stifling a groan. Anne Sloane and John Marshall remained silent and unmoving.

The middle of the big hall was now taken up by a self-contained section. It was easy to imagine how the strangers had brought here all these treasures, many thousands of years ago, to send them into another time era. But were these really treasures?

At first sight the place resembled a storehouse. Boxes and chests stood in neat rows, stacked on top of each other; they formed a border around some object in their center. This object looked quite familiar: it was a matter transmitter!

It must be a medium-sized type; it could accommodate more than one person inside. Its height once again indicated that the unknown race must have been as tall as human beings. The controls of this matter transmitter were similar to those already seen in earlier specimens.

A matter-transmitter—here?

The same question flashed through their minds: where was the anti-transmitter located, the counterpart of this transmitter? What would happen if they entered this transmitter, activated it? Where would they emerge?

Or rather—*when* would they rematerialize?

The inner moon of the 12th planet received sufficient heat from Vega to prevent it from being a totally sterile world. Its own gravitational pull was strong enough to hold a considerable amount of atmosphere trapped above the surface of the moon. It might be conceivable to classify this 12A, as Lossoshér called the satellite, capable of sustaining life.

Sgt. Groll shook his head when the Ferronian scientist asked him to circle slowly around the moon at a low altitude.

"Do you really believe that an immortal race would pick such an inhospitable place to spend the everlasting rest of their lives?"

Lossoshér was crouching in his narrow seat and kept staring out of the view hatch, down on this sparsely lit world. To their left they could see the oversized sphere of the 12th planet. It dominated the scene entirely.

"It does not matter too much what I believe, Sergeant. But we must not overlook anything. We must remember that. This strange race probably regards life differently than we do. Just consider that they seemingly have no other purpose in life than posing riddles for other people. Perhaps they even withdrew into the interior of their own world. If so, you must admit it would not matter at all where this world would be located. It might wander all alone throughout the universe, without a sun, without moons, without light, without heat. Why, then, couldn't it be right here?"

Groll did not reply. He was at a loss what to say.

Seen from above, the 12A was a dead world. The stony desert showed a few rare plant specimens—the only sign of organic life. Here and there, a miserable rivulet squeezed its way through the rocks, soon to ooze away in the dry soil. There were no seas, no oceans. The moon consisted of one uninterrupted land mass. This did not exclude, however, that water might gather deep below the surface, forming underground water reservoirs. Still, this had no influence on the climate of the desolate world above ground.

After they had circled twice around the moon, Lossoshér said: "Let's land here!"

Sgt. Groll cursed under his breath but he remembered the orders Maj. Deringhouse had given him: all wishes of the Ferronian scientist were to be carried out unconditionally.

And he, Sgt. Groll, of all people had to be entrusted with such a task!

The machine descended steadily, flying above the dead landscape at a height of less than a thousand feet.

"Where?"

"Let's wait a little longer," Lossoshér said. His face reflected his intense emotions. It was as if he were searching for something. "Just keep on flying at this altitude. Slow down, please, if you possibly can."

Groll let the fighter plane glide slowly above the rocks. This was the most desolate sight the pilot had ever seen in all his life.

Lossoshér, on the other hand, did not share Groll's distaste for the view. He kept staring intently through the oval window. Nothing seemed to escape his searching eyes.

Two hours later the scientist finally leaned back in his seat.

"I think we can dispense with a landing. I don't believe we will find anything here. Set course on 12B. Maybe we will be luckier there."

Groll breathed a sigh of relief. He threw a galance at the map and seconds later took off into space. The moon sank away below them.

"I think it's all right now for us to enter the crypt, Khrest," said Rhodan. "The generator has removed the barrier. Nothing can happen to us as long as the energy is flowing. And according to your information this should continue for the next few thousand years. That should give us plenty of time. Let's go, then!"

Rhodan walked ahead. Khrest followed after some initial hesitation. Bell waited for a while before he joined them, together with the two mutants. The rest of the members of the mutant corps remained in the background. They did not budge from the spot.

Rhodan reached the place where previously the invisible wall had obstructed his path. Now the obstacle had vanished. There was a heavy trunk in his way. He had to make a slight detour around it. Then he entered the vault.

He stopped in front of the transmitter, the largest object inside the crypt and located right in the center. Rhodan put his hand in his pocket and touched the piece that he kept hidden there. On it was written a mystifying sentence translated by the positronic brain, which had informed him in addition that the same sentence was supposed to make its appearance inside the crypt. It was the beginning of the new trail.

Khrest was standing beside Rhodan. His reddish eyes were filled with uncertainty. His delicate hands were trembling.

"Perry, you aren't going too . . .?"

Rhodan just stared at the Arkonide scientist. There was something very compelling in his gaze. "You wouldn't stop now, would you, Khrest? After having come this close to our goal? I simply can't believe that! The human race behaves quite different; at least, we don't give in so easily, provided it's for a cause that justifies our efforts. The stakes are high enough here. Just think—eternal life!"

"What good would it do you if you should die trying to reach your goal, Perry?"

"That would hardly have been what the unknowns intended for us, Khrest. They left this trace which inevitably must lead to them. And these unknown people did not even risk anything while putting us onto their scent for it will be found and traced only by those who vibrate on the same wavelength. You can count on it that the planet of eternal life will never be found by uncivilized barbarians. Rest assured, Khrest, the unknowns would never lure us into a trap which might prove fatal to us. We will encounter many obstacles, of course, but death is not one of them."

Bell had been unusually silent. Now he spoke. "Who can tell when these mysterious beings set up this transmitter here in this spot? You said it must have been 10,000 years ago when they left this system. Who knows what might have happened in the meantime that they had not reckoned with? We might even land right in the middle of the Vega sun."

Rhodan shook his head. "That's out of the question. You underestimate the intelligence of these beings. They must definitely have been aware of the possibility that it might take centuries or millennia until someone would find the beginning of their trail. They must have considered all potential astronomical changes in their calculations. I am certain they would not make unnecessary risks."

Rhodan stepped closer to the matter transmitter. He opened the wire gate. The controls, some levers and switches, were exactly like those Rhodan knew from those on Ferrol. Nothing different except for one thing:

this transmitter had remained until now in a different time era, either in the past or in the future.

"You will all stay here," Rhodan said with a strained voice. "I am going ahead by myself. If this transmitter functions properly and I land in some safe place, I'll return at once and pick you up to come with me."

"And what will happen if you don't . . . ?" Bell sounded worried.

Rhodan shrugged his shoulders; simply threw a swift glance in Khrest's direction and then stepped inside the cabin, which could easily accommodate five to six persons.

"Once I have disappeared, you will have to wait here," Rhodan said. "Don't do anything that might endanger my return."

Khrest did not seem too pleased with Rhodan's orders. "Wouldn't it make more sense if somebody else . . .?"

"No, Khrest! I am absolutely convinced of the good intentions of these unknown creatures. They *want* their riddle to be solved some day. Shall I disappoint them?"

Khrest was silent.

Rhodan smiled at Khrest and Bell, waved reassuringly at Anne and John—then depressed the lever.

The result was most puzzling: Rhodan neither vanished nor became invisible. He just stood in the wire cage, as if nothing had happened.

The transmitter was not in working order.

The second moon of the 12th planet could have been a twin of the first satellite. They were both exactly alike. A passable atmosphere, very little water, sparse vegetation, rocky ground and bare mountains.

Lossoshér insisted they should land and Sgt. Groll complied with his wishes rather ungraciously. The machine touched ground on a stony plateau. The automatic control instruments indicated that the atmosphere was rather thin. It did not seem advisable to leave the pressurized cabin without a spacesuit. Cursing under his breath, the Ferronian scientist slipped into a gossamer-like coverall and donned a plastic space helmet.

"Wait here for me," requested Lossoshér, and disappeared in the bottom hatch. It had been fixed up as a provisional airlock. Groll locked the hatch hermetically tight and started the exit procedures. The air was sucked off, a vacuum was created. Then the outside hatch opened and the Ferron was tipped out like a parcel onto the ground. He rolled down on the stony surface of the moon 12B. This rough treatment, however, did not dampen his spirits. The gravitation on this moon was considerably less than that of his home planet Ferrol. Nimbly he leapt to his feet and bounded off, quickly getting away from the fighter plane without so much as even looking back once at Groll, who was watching him from behind the plane's window.

"What an unpleasant character!" grumbled the pilot.

The scientist disappeared behind some rocks. He proceeded without a definite plan, relying on what chance would bring. Common sense told him that his chances here were nil to find any hints as to the whereabouts of the missing planet.

Groll was bored, sitting and waiting inside the narrow cabin. He, too, could have gone outside, but he could not see that it would serve any purpose. Thus he just sat and waited.

Two hours later Lossoshér returned. He did not show any signs of disappointment. Slowly he climbed through the airlock into the interior of the plane, took off his space helmet and snorted: "Nothing! This is definitely not the lost planet we are looking for. Let's try the next one."

Groll sighed. "It won't be any different there. How many moons are there around the 13th planet?"

"Only two," replied Lossoshér. There were two deep creases in his high bulging forehead. He gave the impression of concentrating on something important. "And one of the two is rather interesting from an astronomical point of view."

Groll made no comment. He started the engine. Not until 12B was receding rapidly below them did he finally remark: "What's so special about it?"

"This moon is so far away from its planet that it takes half a year for one revolution around it. This makes moon 13B more or less a planet rather than a moon. It's just that it circles around another planet and together with that around the sun. Why shouldn't it be the 43rd planet we are looking for?"

"Why shouldn't it? You have a point there." Groll thought a moment and then added with a grin: "But— on the other hand, why *should* it be the 43rd planet?"

Perry Rhodan tried once more but it was again in vain. Nothing changed. The transmitter seemed dead.

Rhodan stepped out of the wire cage, his disappointment clearly showing on his face. "I can't understand what's wrong there," he admitted to Khrest. "We succeeded in overcoming quite a few obstacles, certainly not just to come to a standstill in front of a defective matter transmitter. What does it mean, I wonder?"

"There must be some meaning to it!" Khrest sounded convinced. "Think of all the other transmitters. None ever suffered any damage throughout the thousands of years. They kept on working in perfect order all the time. The source of their energy supply is inexhaustible. The generators are built-in, as we have learned. Therefore, we must conclude that there must be some reason this transmitter here is not functioning. It must be on purpose. What do you think, Bell?"

Bell did not really have any particular opinion on the subject but he wanted to save face. "I agree with you, Khrest," he began slowly, to gain time. "These beings from the past certainly did not lack imagination. Now, to top it all off, they even want us to repair a matter transmitter to prove our ability to think in five-dimensional terms."

Bell had suggested this more or less because he wanted to say something when he had been challenged by Khrest. But Rhodan seemed to take his words seriously. Rhodan glanced briefly at his friends, then turned his attention to the transmitter again.

He opened the door to the wire cage and stepped inside. Khrest waited, as well as Anne Sloane and John Marshall. Bell, however, who had not failed to notice the unexpected effect of his suggestion, felt encouraged for further explorations.

Rhodan was searching. He was looking for something

definite—the hint that would bring them nearer to the solution of this mystery.

The unknown race possessed an invaluable secret: immortality. They were willing to share this knowledge with a race that would be on a par with them. But how could they make sure who was worthy indeed to learn their secret? The answer was simple: they had to pass a number of tests! Therefore they left behind them a cleverly devised trail when they disappeared. If anyone succeeded in following this trail and interpreting correctly the many hidden hints, then some day the two would have to meet—those who set the task and those who solved it. Those who devised the mystery and those who unraveled it.

A genuine cosmic mystery hunt!

A galactic riddle!

The Galactic Riddle!

Rhodan realized that the transmitter presented two problems at the same time. First, the machine had to be put back into working order and, next, it would transport them to some unknown place, where, however . . .

He did not dare reflect further. Whatever problem would confront them there would be another task to solve.

Suddenly Reginald Bell cried out in surprise. Khrest hurried over to him, joined by the two mutants. It took several seconds before Rhodan could walk over to the group that had gathered around Bell. Rhodan still had his hand in his pocket, grasping the strip of paper which seemed to burn like fire inside his palm.

"What happened? Did you find anything?"

"An inscription!" Bell exclaimed loudly. "I have discovered an inscription. At the back of the transmitter. It was quite simple!"

Rhodan pulled the slip of paper out of his pocket. He looked at it, then compared the text with the two lines inscribed on the otherwise smooth back wall of the transmitter. Then he returned the paper to his pocket.

Bell watched this manoeuver, the disappointment clearly showing on his face. "Was that a dictionary you consulted just now?" he inquired sarcastically.

"Yes, Reg, if you don't mind." Rhodan examined the two lines on the transmitter closely. "These letters are identical with the type we found in the earlier messages. Therefore they must be characters of one and the same language. The language of the immortals. We encountered this same sentence at the very beginning of the trail we have been pursuing. It stands to reason: the transmitter must be the continuation of that trail."

"Sentence? What sentence?" Bell was puzzled.

"This language consists of pictorial symbols, geometrical signs and strange characters. Besides, it is composed in a complicated code, which can be interpreted only by the positronic brain."

"And what is that sentence?" Bell kept insisting.

Rhodan smiled. " 'You will find the light, if your mind corresponds to that of the highest order.' I had the feeling that we would find this message somewhere around here. Now we know for sure that we are on the right track, that will eventually lead us to that light."

Bell kept staring at the strange symbols. "If our mind corresponds to that of the highest order. But does it really, Perry?"

"At least we can be positive that this is the case of the positronic robot's mind!" Rhodan concluded with emphasis.

Moon 12C held no surprises, neither did 13A.

Groll was rather curious as he directed the small fighter plane away from the 13th planet and with increasing speed toward its outer, second moon.

The satellite's diameter was less than that of Mars and its gravitation almost 1G. This fact seemed rather unusual. Lossoshér suggested that this could be explained only if heavy elements composed the interior of the moon. The atmosphere was breathable and not too thin. Lossoshér checked his notes from previous exploratory flights, which told that the climate was rough and cold, but passable.

This moon is really a world, an inhabitable planet, thought Groll. He wondered why the Ferrons had not colonized it. When he expressed his thoughts in a question to the Ferronian scientist, the latter declared: "The climate on 13B is tolerable as far as you are concerned. Our population density is far too small for us to need colonies. And particularly not on such an inhospitable world as moon 13B. It's too cold for us. You see, it is nothing extraordinary that we seem to ignore planets or moons that could be developed as colonies. Perhaps later on if our own planet becomes too small for our needs . . ."

The 13th planet diminished in size while the outer moon began to loom increasingly larger. The shimmering envelope of its atmosphere, illuminated by weak light from the far distant Vega sun, stood out clearly against the darkness of space. Moon 13B would have been considered a planet back home in their own solar system, thought Groll with envy. A far better world than Mars—if Lossoshér had not exaggerated in his data about this satellite. And the heavy interior might indicate that a future mining enterprise might prove profitable.

There were no cloud formations to obstruct the view on the small world's surface. Here too, Groll realized with resignation, were neither oceans nor lakes. That means little water, he thought, feeling disappointed. But at least several smaller rivers in the wide plains. They emptied in deeper lying basins and then oozed away in the ground. This resulted in extensive green areas that seemed to invite potential settlers.

"Didn't the Ferrons send some expeditions to this world?" Groll wondered aloud. "There must be life on such a world."

"Nature is generous," Lossoshér replied. "Many worlds may exist somewhere in the universe, that are only waiting to be discovered by intelligent races. These worlds developed only vegetation, but no sentient, intelligent beings. We do have reports about this moon, of course, but none speaks of the existence of present or past life. However, I believe these observations were not too thorough. I would doubt that anyone ever actually landed on 13B."

"How careless," remarked Groll. "Or maybe, it is rather due to the immense size of your system which contains so many inhabitable worlds. Our own solar system has only two planets in addition to our own which are suitable for settlements."

"Your system is very far from Vega, isn't it?" Lossoshér asked off-handedly. But Groll had not forgotten Rhodan's instructions.

"Whether far or near, what difference does it make?"

The Ferron pretended not to have noticed how his pilot evaded answering his question. The day would come when he would find out where these strangers originated from. Now he suddenly pointed downward.

"You see that mountain range? Try to fly along it at a low altitude. If the immortals left some sign for us, then it must be only at some spot that is easily detected and visible from far away. A mountain top would be the ideal place."

That seemed sensible, and Groll descended lower still, flying above the green plain in the direction of the mountain range.

There were no trees, only tall grass with occasional rocky shelves jutting out. A shallow river serpentined with a thousand little ramifications through a maze of tiny islands. It was a primeval landscape, only the animals were missing. The land lay there lonely, as if waiting for some life to come.

Now the grass was lower and increasingly sparse. Soon there were only occasional tufts on the rocky ground. The character of the landscape changed. It became dry and sterile. Nothing but bare rocks, gently rising higher and higher.

Groll pulled the machine higher up, paralleling the rise of the ground, which kept looming up steeper and steeper, without any irregularities along its surface.

Lossoshér was glued to the window of the plane.

He observed attentively every detail of the terrain, searching for traces he was not sure even existed or what they might look like. For all he knew they might be chasing phantoms.

The slope kept climbing steeply, then suddenly ceased. Groll saw in amazement an even plain stretching to the far horizon. This high plateau was like a different world that had nothing in common with the flat lowlands they had left behind. Its altitude was nearly 6,000 feet. There was no water, no vegetation. It was a dead, hostile land. If ever there had existed a civilization on this moon, then certainly not up here on this plateau.

Lossoshér seemingly paid no attention to this obvious fact. "Pull up a bit higher for a better overall view," he suggested to his pilot. "Watch out for any unusual features."

"Do you really think these immortals placed some signposts for us down there? That's absurd."

"What is regarded as normal by strangers frequently seems absurd to us," argued the scientist. "The same way, of course, the other way round. We must bear this in mind, for those who live longer than the sun certainly must have taken this into account too. What's the reading on your gravometer?"

Groll was startled by Lossoshér's last remark. He looked at the instrument panel and tried to concentrate on this abrupt change of topic.

"There must undoubtedly be heavy elements below. But they might be just naturally occurring in this arrangement. Or do you assume this could be attributed to some subterranean installations of the unknown race?"

"Who knows?" Lossoshér said with an air of mystery. "Wouldn't that be a nice surprise if we could find the entrance to their abode?"

Incorrigible optimist, thought Groll, and cursed this crazy task he had been ordered to carry out. It really could have been fun otherwise, if he had not had to accompany this Ferronian scientist. He could have enjoyed exploring this little world below. He would have landed on the grassy plain, then searched for small animals, or examined the water from the river for protozoa with his microscope and——

"Look at that group of isolated rocks over there!" Lossoshér's request interrupted Groll's pleasant daydreams. "Touch down close by."

Groll said nothing. He simply began the landing manoeuver. He banked and circled low above the irregularly scattered rocks. Then he set the machine gently down next to the largest rock. The terrain looked wild and rugged. Not a trace of life or vegetation.

"The atmosphere is all right for us here. You can accompany me, if you like."

Groll did not accept the invitation. He waited until the scientist had left the plane and disappeared in the maze of rocks. Then he took a light hand raygun from the weapon shelf, checked it briefly, then put the gun in his belt. He stepped from the plane. After all, he wanted to profit from the occasion to go exploring the area a bit on his own.

He closed the exit door, setting the lock for a new combination known to him alone. This way he made sure that nobody could enter the fighter plane without automatically blocking the driving gear.

The air was cool and fresh but seemed to contain insufficient oxygen, for Groll had to breathe rapidly. Like back home on some mountain 12,000 feet high, he thought. Well, that should not present too much of a difficulty for him in his explorations.

Slowly he tried to follow behind Lossoshér, who had been lost from view among the rocks. The terrain was vast and not easy to survey. How absurd to insist on searching here of all places for the remnants of some lost civilization! The ground was smooth and even, except for an occasional boulder which jutted out against the bluish-green sky like rounded-off cones.

Groll was wondering how these odd formations might have come about. After all, there was no water present. Storms would occur only seldom and then not at all violent. Surely this world must have looked quite different in the past. He tried to explain this odd landscape.

The silence around him seemed uncanny. The only sound audible was Groll's footsteps, mulitplied by the echo thrown back from the surrounding rock walls. Somewhere, he could not quie determine where, he could hear other footsteps—those of Lossoshér.

All of a sudden, he stopped and listened closely. He heard now only Lossoshér's steps, but rather indistinct and confusing. The sound came from his right, from his left, from behind him and from the front. Just as if a whole army were marching through the pillars of the rock cones. The echo was reflected from the walls over and over again until it finally reached an exit from this echo chamber in an upward direction.

But the pilot's well-trained ear could very well distinguish between the original footsteps and their echo. It was not easy to do, but not impossible.

Groll's hand wandered automatically over to his belt, feeling for his gun. The cool metal felt reassuring.

There were other steps besides those of the Ferronian scientist—slow, cautiously groping, creeping steps.

Groll and Lossoshér were not alone on this world.

3 THE LURKING DANGER

THEY had called it a day and no longer pursued their attempt to return the matter transmitter to proper working order. Khrest had thoroughly examined the transmitter and found out that the connections had been deliberately broken in some places. There were also some faulty installations that would cause short circuits.

"This is our first task, which we must solve before we can continue with our other experiments," Khrest summed up the situation. Then he added: "Fortunately we have in our possession the construction plans for the transmitter. With the help of our positronic brain we will obtain a circuit diagram. Let's hope that one of our properly programmed worker robots will be able to correct the faulty installations that the unknowns seem to have put here on purpose."

Rhodan judged it best to go along with Khrest's suggestions. They had left one of the mutants behind in the vault to keep guard over the matter transmitter. The neutralizing generator remained switched on for they certainly did not wish to risk that the crypt might disappear again into the secrecy of time.

Rhodan spent half the night in the center which housed the big Arkonide positronic brain, that was a little brother of the gigantic positronic installation on Venus, where it had been left behind by the ruling race of the universe. This had been during the era when Atlantis existed on Earth. Rhodan fed his questions nonstop into the positronic brain, which spat out formula after formula in reply. Rhodan compared the answers. The simultranslators gave instructions over the loudspeakers.

Rhodan kept up a dialogue with the positronic brain as if it were a living being. He put his questions to it and the brain in return supplied the desired information. Seen from a positronic point of view the brain was certainly alive, and in any case it was far more intelligent than any of the organic life forms in the universe.

Rhodan did not stop until the simplified diagram of connections was in his hands and the positronic brain had confirmed most of the conjectures he had formed about the game of riddle-solving the immortals had thought up. Finally Rhodan felt satisfied. He felt certain he was on the track of the greatest mystery of the universe. He would not rest until he unraveled it.

The next morning Khrest conditioned one of the worker robots who specialized in positronics. His synthetic thought processes were readjusted on a five-dimensional basis. Then the robot received its instructions by being connected directly to the big positronic brain in the *Stardust*. It took 10 minutes for the robot, which had been fashioned after an Arkonide model, to become the most perfect constructor of matter transmitters of the present time. It would be a simple task for it to repair any defective transmitter.

Including those that had been put out of commission on purpose, using the most refined ruses.

Rhodan waited until afternoon before he returned

to Thorta. He had hoped to receive some news from Sgt. Groll but no communication had arrived from the fighter plane. There was no reason to be unduly concerned about this silence. Lossoshér might be so involved in his search that he might forget to make an intermediary report. Or the silence could mean that the two men had not yet found a trace of the lost race of the immortals.

The Thort's bodyguards could hardly conceal their astonishment when Rhodan, Khrest, Bell and the worker robot stepped out of the official transmitter inside the Red Palace. The Ferrons had never before seen such a perfect metallic imitation of a man.

Down below in the vault nothing had changed. The robot set to work immediately under the supervision of his masters. Within a few minutes he had exposed the inner workings of the transmitter. The confusion of electronic miniaturized instruments and plastic conduits might have discouraged Rhodan under normal circumstances. But here he knew that the limitless knowledge of the positronic brain was standing behind him in the shape of the worker robot. Rhodan remained calm and confident.

"I hope he'll make it, Perry." Bell sounded not too convinced. But Rhodan waved him off with an impatient gesture of his hand. Bell withdrew into the background, slightly unhappy. Khrest, however, watched intently, a confident smile playing around his lips while the worker robot kept up a steady pace removing the faulty connections and replacing them with new ones.

The long minutes grew into an hour which seemed to last an eternity to the men.

Finally the robot closed the magnetic snap lid over the interior working mechanism of the transmitter and announced in a monotone: "The transmitter is again ready for use."

Rhodan breathed a sigh of relief. He glanced at Bell, rewarded the exiting robot with a friendly slap on his bare, metallic shoulder, then inquired of Khrest: "When?"

"This is what I have been asking myself the whole time, Perry. Probably tomorrow. We must first carefully work out the composition of the group that will go on this hazardous mission. Who knows, we might land inside another transmitter, whose receiving mechanism functions perfectly alright while its sending installations have been tampered with, just like this one here. I insist on taking along the repair robot. Also a physician. Dr. Haggard would be the ideal person for this."

"And in addition to him, the two mutants Sloane and Marshall." Rhodan agreed to Khrest's suggestion. "With such a group we can face any difficulty that we may encounter. This leap into the unknown will lead us to the next task. I am confident we will be able to solve it."

Khrest kept his eyes fixed on a spot on the floor. After a few moments of silent meditation, he looked at Rhodan. "I still have some doubts about the whole enterprise, Perry. I feel it is presumptuous on our part to attempt to delve into the secrets of a great race."

"We are not guilty of any indiscretion, Khrest. After all, they deliberately planted that trail for us to follow."

"That's just a hypothesis, Perry. We don't know this

to be a fact. To my mind we are risking our lives if we try playing their games."

"Quite the contrary, Khrest—and the positronic brain is of the same opinion. Do you really believe it makes more sense to look for the lost planet at random anywhere in the universe?"

"Sometimes I am convinced it would be better to give up this search as a lost cause. It is hopeless."

Bell had been fretting in the background. It was hard for him to listen passively to this discussion. Now he gathered up sufficient courage, especially since he knew that Perry Rhodan shared his point of view in this matter, and remarked in a chiding tone: "Khrest, I can't understand such an attitude. Who would give up the chance to gain eternal life? Don't you see, immortality is the prize that the unknown race is holding out for us if we solve the great riddle?"

"You are just assuming all this, my friend," Khrest said gently. "I admit even our original expedition from Arkon was based on nothing but assumptions and ancient reports. The planet of eternal life *is supposed* to exist, but that was 10,000 years ago."

"Excellent!" said Rhodan. "This is the evidence that our theories must be right. We already have absolute proof that an alien race stayed in this system some 10,000 years ago. And according to their own statements this race 'lives longer than the sun.' This is the same as being immortal in human eyes. It stands to reason this race must be identical with the one which lived on your planet of eternal life. Thus we have the beginning of the trail. And to follow this trail is the actual original task of your own research expedition, Khrest."

The Arkonide was still hesitating. "Of course you are right there, Perry. Forgive me for expressing my doubts, for presenting such spurious arguments. You are too fast for me, Perry; you make such rapid decisions. The Arkonides will *think* fast, but *act* slowly . . ."

"So slow that your galactic empire goes to wrack and ruin!" interrupted Bell, brutally.

Khrest no longer smiled but his eyes were full of gentle forbearance. "Well, then, tomorrow, if this will suit you. I am happy that we have finally come to an agreement. Let's go and get a good night's rest!"

Sgt. Groll stood rooted to the ground.

It is an odd sensation to be on an uninhabited planet and suddenly to encounter another living being. Especially if you have no idea who this other "person" might be.

While Groll stood listening for the steps of the stranger, his thoughts were racing wildly. His head was filled with all kinds of speculation. A living creature here on 13B? Could it be that Lossoshér was right after all? Was the unknown race indeed living here on this moon? Those unknowns that once upon a time had made a gift to the Ferrons—the matter transmitter —and then had withdrawn to some unknown destination? Could it be true that they had brought their own planet to this place in the system, and then disguised it as a moon of the 13th planet?

And—were they vicious?

Groll's hand moved instinctively to his belt. The

heavy butt-end of his raygun felt reassuring to his touch. The question still remained if this weapon could be effectively used against beings who thought in a fifth-dimensional manner. Beings that were capable of building matter transmitters. The unknowns who could impose their will on an entire planet and displace it from its original orbital path.

His heart was heavy with doubts but he did not lose courage. Besides, he suddenly realized that he might turn out to be one of the most important members of Rhodan's space expedition. What if he should be so fortunate and discover the hiding place of those un-knowns they were looking for——

Lossoshér apparently had stopped. Groll could no longer hear his footsteps. For a moment he could hear the faint echo of the creeping steps of Lossoshér's pursuer, then everything became quiet. Only a gentle wind rustled through the rock pillars.

Cold shudders ran down Groll's back. His fingers grasped tightly the butt-end of the weapon that he had pulled out of his belt. His thumb lay on the trigger. He did not dare move, fearing this might draw the unknown's attention to him. He still had the advan-tage of the element of surprise. The unknown evidently must think that he was facing only one adversary: the Ferron.

However, Groll could not remain inactive. He was responsible for the scientist's safety. And Lossoshér was unarmed.

Sgt. Groll plucked up courage and began to move. First one cautious step. He was not sure which direc-tion to choose but he supposed that Lossoshér and the unknown stranger must be behind the next rocky cone. The scientist certainly paid no heed to what else might be going on around him, as he was searching for the remains of a lost civilization while a living enemy was creeping toward him.

Groll's hand tightened around the gun. He made another step forward. He was careful not to make any noise. The ground was even and it was easy to walk around the occasional little heaps of rubble in his path, in order to avoid stumbling over a small stone.

The blood almost froze in his veins when he heard a shout of surprise very close by. It must be Lossoshér. But he did not call out in fear; on the contrary his voice sounded triumphant. Groll was at a loss; he did not understand this.

Then once more the strong, firm steps of the Ferron. Groll heard stones being moved and rolled aside. The echo resounded from the rocky walls. In between came the sound of the laboured breathing of the hard-working scientist. Lossoshér was talking to himself all the while, but it was impossible for Groll to understand even a single word. However it was easy to guess that the scientist had made some thrilling discovery and had become entirely oblivious to his surroundings.

The pilot inched his way around the rock pillar that obstructed his way, keeping virtually glued to the smooth stone. He saw now how the narrow path widened into a small plateau that was bounded by steep walls. The distant Vega sun was very low in the sky, its rays just barely touching the tops of the highest pillars. It grew rapidly darker.

But it was still light enough to recognize Lossoshér,

who was busy moving big boulders with his bare hands, trying to clear a structure that was half buried underneath the rocks. Groll could just make out the very top of the building. Seen from the distance it appeared to be a pyramid.

Lossoshér was working hard, rolling the stones aisde. Now Groll could see the smooth walls of the pyramid. Its even surface was broken only in the center by some kind of an inscription. Lossoshér concentrated on removing the rubble to lay bare the writing.

About 10 yards away from Lossoshér was another rock pillar with a gaping, dark, half-round opening, the entrance to a tunnel. The last weak rays of the sun permitted Groll to make out that the floor of this corridor fell away at a steep angle about six feet away from the entrance.

Obviously Lossoshér must have overlooked this entrance or he would not have given his undivided attention to the pyramid.

Groll was just about to call out to the scientist when he remembered the hidden stranger. He had almost forgotten him in the excitement of watching Lossoshér's discovery. Now the raygun in his hand made him once more aware of the lurking danger.

Where was this unknown creature whose creeping steps he had heard a little while ago? Was it sitting in some hiding place busy observing what Lossoshér was doing? What if it had also detected him as he was standing, closely pressed against the rocky wall? And if not, why did it remain so quiet now?

Cautiously Groll started to move ahead, staying close to the wall. Between him and the opposite wall of the narrow gorge was an empty space almost 20 yards wide. Lossoshér and the pyramid were about 30 yards away, and the entrance to the tunnel farther still.

Groll came to a little nook. He stopped. He was fully covered here from all directions. If he were to advance any farther he would lose this advantageous position. Why not remain here and continue observing Lossoshér from this distance? The unknown enemy—provided it really was an enemy—would only concentrate on the Ferron. The opponent would have to give himself away at some time. And then Groll would act accordingly.

It grew almost totally dark now. The last sun rays disappeared. Soon the first stars became visible in the sky. Lossoshér did not seem to notice these changes around him; he was obsessed by his find. Not until he had pushed aside the last obstructing boulder, bending over the mysterious inscription in order to decipher it, did he become aware that it was too dark to read. He had no flashlight on him. He cursed softly and straightened up again, standing and hesitating over what to do next. For a few seconds his figure loomed like a dark shadow against the still brighter walls of the rocks. The 13th planet rose above the horizon, providing just sufficient light to recognize Lossoshér's shadowy outlines.

And it was a shadow that made an end to Groll's passive waiting.

Close by he heard a noise. The unknown must have been standing at the same rock, hardly 10 feet away from him, silently observing Lossoshér all the time.

Now once again the stealthily advancing steps—then

all of a sudden Groll could see a dark figure standing out against the faintly illuminated rocky wall. The shape was larger than life size, its outlines resembling vaguely those of a human being. Yet the pointed head and the shimmering armour evoked horrible memories of an era long gone on Earth and at the same time recently come alive again in the Vega system.

But Groll was not quite sure of himself. Although it was against Rhodan's principles to judge any alien by his outer appearance, and although Groll had been schooled to be unprejudiced, he was almost paralyzed with fright.

Incapable of moving, he remained standing in the safety of the niche, grasping his gun for protection. He tried hard to pierce the darkness in order to see better. Lossoshér was still hesitating, his upright figure outlined against the lighter background. He seemed resigned to having to return to the space fighter plane. He did not see the strange, weird-looking shadow, although it was less than 10 feet away from him.

Groll came to life again.

If he hesitated any longer, the hazy figures of the scientist and the stranger would blend into each other and Groll would not be able to distinguish them. And this would condemn him to inactivity, make him unable to come to the Ferron's assistance.

Groll raised the raygun and pointed at the stranger's shadow. He kept his eyes fixed on it while he called out:

"Lossoshér! Watch out! Run to the right. A stranger is creeping toward you! Hurry!"

Groll did not intend shooting at an alien life form

as long as it had not been identified beyond a doubt to be hostile toward him. The last thing he would want to do would be to start a war with the inhabitants of this planet—he had difficulty regarding 13B as a moon. Of course, the inhabitants were fully entitled to check out any intruders in their territory.

Fortunately for Groll something happened that made such a decision superfluous.

The mighty shadow in the middle of the plateau ceased moving ahead toward Lossoshér. Groll expected at any moment to see the flash from some weapon. He was determined to answer this fire. But all remained quiet.

While the Ferron hesitated just a second before he followed Groll's instructions and ran quickly out of the presumed line of fire, the stranger seized the opportunity to duck and run.

Groll's attention had been diverted for an instant by the Ferron's movements, although he still kept his eyes on the stranger's shadow. But this slight diversion was enough.

Rocks and stones were spattering in all directions as the unknown scurried as fast as a weasel toward the rock pillar with the entrance to the tunnel. It disappeared instantly into the depth of the rocky shelter. Groll could still hear the noises coming from the shaft but they rapidly died down, growing more distant; then all was silent.

Groll waited almost a minute before he called to the Ferron: "He is gone; come here! Let's get back to the ship. Who knows what other dangers are lurking here in the dark?"

The Ferronian scientist came running across the plateau. He did not seem to realize the danger he had barely escaped a little while ago. He was very excited as he said loudly and triumphantly to Groll: "I have found it! I have found those that live longer than the sun!"

Groll felt annoyed. He put the raygun back in his holster.

"A fat lot of good that would do you as a dead man!"

The Ferron seemed startled by this remark. "What do you mean by that? That stranger? Unimportant! Probably just some poor guy out for a walk. He got scared by us and ran."

Groll walked ahead.

He murmured: "Symbolically speaking, the sun does not live here for very long."

4 STRANGER IN A STRANGE TUNNEL

ANOTHER night went by.

Rhodan was determined to solve this day the second part of the cosmic puzzle. He assembled the people he had selected to participate in this venture and pointed out to them the risks they were facing. Then via a matter transmitter they transferred by the fastest and the most convenient way possible directly to the Red Palace of the Thort.

The robot guard did not seem to have budged from the spot since they had left him.

"Nothing to report, sir," he announced when queried by Rhodan.

Bell stepped up to the metallic figure fashioned in the image of their Arkonide masters and with a friendly pat on its cold shoulder he asked: "You mean to say then that it won't be any special risk for us to enter this transmitter and have ourselves carried off to some place?"

"The matter transmitter is in perfect working order, ready at your service," the robot replied without directly answering Bell's question.

"Since you are coming along with us on this trip we have nothing to worry about," grinned Bell. "If you weren't absolutely sure that this thing here is working all right, you would not be willing to run any risks for your own safety's sake."

The robot gave no answer.

Rhodan hesitated a few moments before he entered the transmitter. He was the first to do so. Then his friends followed, Khrest, Haggard and the two mutants, Anne Sloane and John Marshall. Bell let the robot pass in front of him to enter the cage.

It was a tight squeeze inside the narrow confines of the wire cage. An indescribable, eerie feeling came over them. They were all aware that this venture represented a challenge to the past.

Rhodan's hand gripped the lever. It was the same type they knew from the other transmitters they had operated so many times. Their destination had been predetermined for them. This transmitter was the sender and somewhere the receiver that belonged to it must await them.

"Our feelings of apprehension are easy to understand but they are not justified," Rhodan said to his friends. "The positronic brain's deliberations, which as you know are based on infallible logic, state that we are not threatened by any direct danger. We are simply pursuing a trail which was laid many thousand years ago. We don't know how long this trail will be and where it will lead us. We don't know either how many way-stations there are along this road. A superior intellect has puzzled out these problems which we must solve in order to meet their originators. The light they are speaking of is the conservation of cells, which equals eternal life."

"Although I have decided to accompany you on this mission," Khrest remarked in an uncertain voice, "I did it merely out of a sense of duty. I owe this much to my own race. But I must admit that I do not share your optimism."

"You mistrust your own creation, the positronic brain, Khrest? It was not I who worked out the procedures we are to follow, it was the brain that recommended it as the end result of its logical deliberations. And the brain can never be wrong."

"Agreed. However it can make relative mistakes in case the data it has been fed are wrong. Then the conclusion it arrives at must be wrong too. What information do we have about the mentality of those beings that posed the big riddle for us?"

"Quite a lot, Khrest. They must have been endowed with a great sense of humor, that's for sure. And they must have been highly intelligent. And they were, and even still are, friendly to a certain extent, for otherwise they would not be inclined to share their secret with others. The riddle is nothing but some kind of insurance. I have pointed that out to you repeatedly, Khrest, and it is time that you finally believe me. We can reach our goal only if the conditions are right, namely: our intelligence must be of the same quality and level as theirs. And I am confident that this is the case."

"Sure, sure," muttered Bell. "At least I hope it is. I am not too happy about it, though, to be frank. Honestly, I have made my peace with the Lord, as the old saying goes."

"That doesn't sound like you, Reg," Rhodan said. His hand was still resting motionless on the activating lever. "Did you get cold feet all of a sudden?"

"On the contrary," Bell answered with a feeble grin. "The ground is burning under my feet."

Haggard remained silent and so did Anne and John. They had absolute confidence in Rhodan's judgment. Whatever he decided was all right with them. He would not undertake anything light-heartedly. His presence spelled safety for them.

The robot was silent too. This was not unusual, however. Bell was of the opinion that a robot was incapable of experiencing any emotions. Yet there were some moments when he began to have doubts.

"Ready?" Rhodan asked.

All nodded a silent "yes."

Rhodan's jaw line firmed up, his lips narrowed. His eyes were filled with a light of resolute expectation. And then, with a firm motion he depressed the lever.

In contrast to the usual travels with the matter transmitter, they experienced at once a sensation that was totally unfamiliar to them. Stabbing and gnawing pains coursed through their brains, then passed with agonizing slowness down along their spinal columns. Everything grew hazy in front of their eyes; their thought processes ceased entirely.

In reality, all this lasted only a fraction of a second—or was it an eternity? Then, suddenly, it was all over. Their thinking ability returned; the pain vanished; they could see once again.

"Oh, blast it all!" Bell was cursing loudly. He was clinging to the robot's solid form. "Some fun! That's the last time I'm going on such a trip!"

"And how do you imagine you will get back again, Reg?" said Rhodan. "Where are we?"

"You are asking *me*?" Bell tried to pierce the twilight around them with his eyes. They were still standing inside the transmitter cage but they realized it was not the same transmitter they had entered a few seconds earlier. It must be the receiving station.

They had rematerialized again inside some building. The air was very stuffy. It must have been ages since the air had been renewed. There was a dim light coming from some concealed source.

Rhodan opened the gate of the transmitter cage. The same instant everything grew bright around them. The hidden light sources increased in intensity. The men did not move. They waited; they wanted to find their bearings first.

The transmitter was standing in the center of a gigantic hall. They could not locate any exits. The room was cluttered with machines and all kinds of strangely formed objects. There was hardly any free space in this huge area. Narrow passages led through the maze of mysterious machinery whose purpose was beyond their comprehension.

"Let's go!" Rhodan ordered with a strained voice. He was the first to step out of the cage onto the even floor of the hall. "I wonder where we will find our next task?"

As if in answer to his question an inscription lit up all of a sudden on the high ceiling of the room. It was the same writing they had all seen before—strange symbols, hieroglyphics. But even before Rhodan was capable of looking properly at the first letter, the inscription grew dark and entirely disappeared. Rhodan was shocked as he realized he had missed his chance. The inscription had been a clue, a part of the solution of the riddle. He blamed himself for not having thought of bringing a camera along. Since he could not register lightning fast impressions, let alone remember them, he should have thought of such an eventuality and have provided for it. But now it was too late. It seemed senseless to proceed any further.

John Marshall, the esper, intercepted Rhodan's thoughts. "Don't despair," Marshall tried to cheer Rhodan up. "They surely haven't lured us this far only to let us turn back again with nothing achieved. Even if we should never learn the meaning of that inscription—provided they won't repeat it for us somewhere—there will certainly be other tasks awaiting us."

"The symbols will be deciphered by the positronic brain," interjected Khrest. "One of us will have to bring it back and the teleporter Ras Tschubai can pick up the decoded message with a few minutes."

"You seem to forget," Rhodan sounded very bitter, "that the writing has vanished. How can we have something deciphered that no longer exists?"

For the first time since they had started out on their venture Khrest smiled. It was a gentle yet lofty smile. "You have forgotten something, too, Perry. Namely, my eidetic memory. Would you like me to write down that sentence that was visible for just an instant on the ceiling of this hall?"

Rhodan took a deep breath. "Sorry, Khrest. I had really forgotten for a moment. Please, write the sentence on this piece of paper here. The robot will return with it to Thorta. We have no idea how important it will be for us to have it deciphered. Maybe we need it to advance further."

In the meantime all had left the transmitter and stood amidst the gigantic installations which appeared to have been arranged without any obvious purpose. There was no sign of any life around the hall. All were under the impression that they had been transported for no good reason to this subterranean energy plant by the unknowns, who now were waiting for the men's reaction to this move.

They noticed a draught of fresh air suddenly coming from a grille on the ceiling. The place was air conditioned, based on the basal metabolism of oxygen breathers.

"Where are we?" Anne Sloane asked timidly. "On Ferrol?"

"We might be on Ferrol, or even in Thorta," Rhodan replied with a voice that betrayed his uncertainty. "But it might just as well be some planet suspended in space several thousand light-years away. Think of the long-lasting pain during the teleportation. This would indicate a vast distance. But wherever we are, the transmitter station will bring us back again to our starting point, whenever we want it." Rhodan turned to Khrest. "Yes, Khrest?"

"This was the illuminated inscription on the ceiling." Khrest handed Rhodan a piece of paper. "The only one able to decipher it is the positronic brain. Perhaps it would be better to wait before we send off the robot, don't you agree?"

Rhodan hesitated. "I doubt we will find our way around here in this labyrinth of technological marvels. The inscription might supply some hint what we are supposed to do here."

"And what happens if we should need the robot in the meantime?" It was Bell speaking.

"Who else should go? You perhaps?"

"By myself? Alone in this transmitter? No!"

"Well, that settles the question." Rhodan turned to the silently waiting robot. "Take this piece of paper and hurry to the positronic brain in the *Stardust*. Have the inscription deciphered and return with the decoded text. Do this as quick as possible."

"Didn't you want to send Ras Tschubai . . . ?"

"The robot is faster." Rhodan cut short Bell's objections.

Without a word the robot walked over to the transmitter and went inside. With mixed feelings the men who remained behind saw it disappear seconds later.

"This inscription was not the only clue we were supposed to find here," began Rhodan. "The purpose of this maze of technical installations cannot merely be intended to distract us. The tests will become progressively harder, you can be sure of that. Let's go. But stay close together at all times, to keep our action potential unimpaired. Khrest has already had to give proof of his abilities. We don't know who will be next."

He started to move ahead. Khrest followed with Haggard. Then came Anne and John, while Bell brought up the rear. Bell glanced longingly at the transmitter, reflecting whether it would not have been wiser after all if he had left instead of the robot.

From somewhere came a humming sound.

It was a low, regular hum as if a motor had been started. Who had started the motor? No one was to be seen. The entire installation—in case it really was an installation—must be operated automatically. But where? And by whom?

The humming came from the right. Rhodan took the next turn in the passage and walked toward the noise. He knew he had no other choice in order to avoid wasting time. And time, he guessed, was the most important factor planted here thousands of years ago.

The shimmering metal of the strange machines seemed to radiate a message of taunting threat. Bell once accidentally brushed against one of the heavy metal blocks. He winced as if he had touched a snake.

The hum originated from a square metal housing at the end of the corridor. Rhodan stopped in front of the cube and examined it. He felt as if probing fingers were suddenly exploring his brain. Something alien was trying to tell him something. But what?

"Marshall, do you notice it too?"

The telepath nodded silently. His eyes were closed and he seemed to listen to some inner voice. Sweat beaded his forehead. Khrest also stood stock still. Bell, however, over to the side, was not affected at all by the strange phenomenon. He just kept hearing the humming and tried to find an explanation for it. All the metal cube meant to him was simply another one of the numerous machines or generators.

Suddenly the humming sound ceased. Dead silence reigned in the hall.

Rhodan felt the probing fingers in his brain grow faint and vanish completely. John Marshall breathed a sigh of relief. He opened his eyes again.

"It was a telepathic message," he said. "This machine is a probing mechanism of mental structures. It has examined our intellectual abilities and our intelligence quotients. The result was positive—at least partially."

"What is that supposed to mean?"

"The instrument detected in us various reactions, far as I could make out. The end result is favorable, however it stated that Bell, Haggard and Miss Sloane were lacking telepathic abilities. It discovered in you, Rhodan, as well as in Khrest, rudimentary forms of telepathic capacities. As far as I am concerned, it regarded me as being of high calibre and therefore informed me of the result of its examinations."

"That eludes me," said Bell. "That machine had a conversation with you?"

"If you want to put it that way, yes. I could understand what it was thinking. In any case, we have passed the test successfully. We are supposed to continue searching."

"Searching? Searching for what?"

"The telepathic automaton did not give any indication what it might be."

Rhodan was about to reply when formidable bolts of lightning shot across the room, followed shortly by ear-splitting discharges. The lightning came from a bluish, glistening sphere which was hovering, without any visible support, just below the ceiling. The lightning arced across a distance of over 10 yards and touched another sphere which was fastened by a small antenna onto a huge metal casing.

Over 10 yards! That meant 10 million volts!

The globe on the receiving end began to glow and turned white, radiating waves of constantly rising temperatures. A strong odour of ozone filled the air. Then the lightning bolts ceased. The globe, however, continued to glow. The subterranean room heated up rapidly.

"What was that?" Bell's voice had lost its usual self-assurance.

"A rather drastic demonstration of wireless transfer of energy, if I am not mistaken," suggested Rhodan. "Not much practical use for it, though. I don't know what we are supposed to do with it. If that should be some new task . . ."

Once more he could not finish what he had to say. He was interrupted again.

They heard a commotion somewhere within the giant installation. Steps were coming closer, firm, hefty steps, approaching with an even, monotonous rhythm.

Khrest, who was standing next to Rhodan, grew pale. He started trembling all over. Bell could not help noticing this with a touch of gloating satisfaction; but almost immediately he, too, was overcome by fear and could hardly hide his consternation.

Rhodan's body stiffened. A tense expression came over his face. He paid no attention to his companions and did not seem to be aware that Marshall's hand flew with a reflex movement to his pocket.

Somebody—or something—came toward them from the vast hall filled with a jungle of machinery. It still remained invisible. Now the steps seemed to approach from behind. The same firm, unswerving steps.

"Don't do anything hasty!" Rhodan whispered to his companions. He looked sternly at Marshall. "They can't be any real enemies. Show no signs of fear. The galactic game of riddle-solving is a matter of intelligence

76

and prestige."

Now they sighted a figure coming around a corner of the narrow corridor between the lines of machines. The figure was still far away. It looked almost human, although taller and heftier, except for the missing legs. Instead it had two high wheels. The torso was oddly angular yet symmetrical. There were strangely shaped antennae and feelers sprouting from its head. Its eyes were illuminated by a glow coming from inside.

"It's a robot," Khrest whispered. "It's not alive the same way we are. Could it have been that robots . . ."

"Nonsense!" Rhodan spoke sharply. Now they could clearly hear the stomping sound that they had mistaken for steps. This rhythmical pounding emanated from inside the robot's body, which towered seven feet tall. Could this noise come from some engine in its interior? Was it some diversionary manoeuver? It did not seem to make any sense.

Another robot appeared from behind and approached rapidly.

Rhodan quickly sized up the situation. The massive blocks of machinery surrounded them from all sides. They were so close together that it would be impossible to slip between them in order to escape. Neither could they climb up on the high smooth walls of these metal cubes. Unless these robots stopped in time . . .

Rhodan decided to make an attempt at stopping them. "You stay here," he ordered his friends. Then he walked toward the first robot. The monster moved relatively slowly but steadily. Probably some mechanism had been activated when Rhodan and his group penetrated this hall. A mechanism that had been waiting, ready for instant action at the proper time, for many thousands of years. And now it was their task to immobilize this mechanism once more.

Rhodan stopped five yards in front of the giant. It was not a sight to inspire confidence. From both eyes radiated a glow of some barely contained energy. Delicate, silvery feelers played nervously, reaching out to Rhodan as if they expected something from him. A metal rod on the robot's head began to vibrate. And all the time the mighty wheels kept turning, advancing the machine at a steady pace. There was no indication that this forward movement would cease.

With an instinctive gesture Rhodan stretched out both hands, as if trying to halt the machine. He commanded: "Stop!"

The robot kept on rolling forward.

Without any further attempt Rhodan retreated to his waiting friends.

"Marshall, issue a telepathic order! Maybe he'll react to that."

The telepath nodded silently and advanced. Meanwhile the threat from the second robot had become more acute as it kept coming closer from behind. The structure made of unknown alloys and activated by some mysterious electronic forces approached inexorably as if its counterpart on the other side were exerting some magical attraction. Both giants seemed determined to meet regardless of whatever lay in their path, mowing down without pity any obstacles barring their way.

Anne Sloane felt desperate that she was unable to help her friends despite her special gifts as a mutant.

Now she found the only possible way out. For why should she not be able to come to everyone's rescue? Why did this solution not occur to Rhodan right away?

Without saying a word, she walked toward the robot coming from behind them. She came to a halt a few steps before the giant figure. Summoning the strength she had trained for during many years, she forced her mind to intense concentration. She knew that her abilities would be tested in a manner as never before. And yet, from a technical point of view all was so simple. It was only her fear of potential failure that threatened to paralyze her strength. At the same time, her mortal fright had just the opposite effect.

Anne Sloane's mental energies concentrated into a beam which she directed against the robot. They hit it like the rays of a powerful invisible spotlight.

Rhodan was busy observing Marshall's unsuccessful attempts at stopping the advancing robot via telepathic commands. He paid no attention to Anne's endeavours. Only Bell turned around and watched the young girl. He enjoyed a truly unique spectacle!

The robot appeared to have run into an invisible wall. The wheels began to spin briefly, then stood still. There was the stench of burned-out insulation in the heavy air, which kept getting hotter and hotter from the constantly glowing globe.

The passage was rather narrow. It was totally blocked by the immobilized robot. There was no chance for Rhodan's group to squeeze by and escape. Although the obstacle had been brought to a stand still it had not been removed. Besides, it was no great help if only one of the robots had been stopped, as long as the other one was rolling steadily toward the group. Unfortunately it was impossible for the young telekineticist to arrest the advance of both machines simultaneously.

Anne Sloane was thinking furiously. Before Bell managed to give any advice she had already found the only possible solution out of the dilemma.

Once more she increased her endeavours by channeling her streams of thoughts. The concentrated energies of her mind changed into positive kinetic energy—and lifted the robot off the ground.

Its wheels began to spin anew while the metal monster drifted slowly upward. Five inches, then 10 inch —finally two feet.

Anne Sloane felt her strength give way. How long could she maintain this effort? But she simply had to! Unless she could manage to remove this obstacle from their path and render it harmless, they would all be lost.

Now the robot was floating two yards, then three above the floor of the room. It had reached the top rim of the machine cubes. But Anne Sloane was still not satisfied. She kept raising the colossus until it was just below the ceiling, more than five yards above the upper surface of the machine structures. Now a little bit to the side, two, three yards . . .

And then she let go.

With spinning wheels the robot hung for a fraction of a second above the metal mass of the machines before it began to fall. And then the clattering noise as metal crashed hard on metal.

The sudden sound of breaking and splintering startled Rhodan and the others and made them turn around. Even Marshall forgot his senseless efforts to make the robot obey his telepathic commands. He whirled around just in time to see the outside body of the second attacker smash to smithereens on top of the huge cube. The same moment, he as well as the rest of the group noticed Anne Sloane slump to the ground before anyone could jump to her assistance. The strain had been too great for the slender girl.

Rhodan sized up the situation instantly. "Back to the transmitter!" he yelled, no longer paying any attention to the first robot, which kept steadily rolling forward. "Hurry, before it gets to us!"

Marshall pulled a raygun out of his pocket. Nobody knew that he had brought along this weapon. "Shall I destroy it?"

"No!" shouted Rhodan. "Our tasks can never be accomplished by sheer violence. You'd better help me carry Anne. Get a move on, Bell. Give us a hand!"

They retreated quickly but in an orderly fashion. During these few moments Rhodan was busy evaluating their failure in carrying out their mission. They had definitely failed, he was sure of that. And it could all have been so simple, if looked at properly. Anne Sloane's telekinetic powers were insufficient to overcome two adversaries simultneously. But they did actually have *two* telekinetics. After all, there was still Betty Toufry.

The thought of Betty made Rhodan's heart beat faster. Why hadn't he thought of her earlier? The little girl who had just turned nine was a parapyschological wonder. She had mastered the art of telepathy better than any member of the mutant corps. Despite her youth she had even outpaced Anne Sloane.

"If we can manage to get Betty Toufry here in time," panted Rhodan, while running around the last turn, "all might not be lost yet. As long as we can stop that robot before it reaches the transmitter. I'm sure it is scheduled to destroy our transmitter, to cut us off from our only means of escape and prevent us from returning. It has not yet won this battle; there is still hope for us!"

They had reached the cage. But before Rhodan had time to give any orders, all saw the Arkonide robot materialize inside the transmitter—and then another figure, a very small, slender shape!

Nobody spoke a word as Betty Toufry stepped out of the transmitter cage. She seemed somewhat embarrassed. Fear clouded her face as she noticed Anne Sloane's unconscious form held in Bell's arms. Marshall stood over to the side, undecided whether he should concentrate on the unconscious girl or the giant robot that kept unerringly rolling toward them.

Rhodan had gotten over his initial surprise. "Betty, you are coming as if you had heard me call you," he stated, and glanced at Khrest as if to question him. But the Arkonide apparently was at a loss for an explanation. "Anne Sloane can't make it on her own. We are being attacked by a giant robot. You must put it out of action. Anne Sloane simply lifted up the first attacking robot and then let it drop."

"The positronic brain gave me the advice," said the Arkonide robot with its inanimate metallic voice, "to bring along the mutant Betty Toufry. Perhaps it concluded this as a necessary means upon receiving this message." With these words the robot handed Rhodan a slip of paper.

With a flash Rhodan remembered that he had originally sent the robot up—why he was thinking in terms of "up" and "down" was not clear to Rhodan at this moment—in order to have the mysterious symbols of the illuminatd inscription decoded by the positronic brain.

And now he could read the decoded message: *Welcome to the center of a thousand tasks—but only a single one of these will bring you closer to your goal.*

That was all. The meaning was clear. Rhodan expressed it. "One thousand tasks are awaiting us. We almost failed while trying to solve the second or third of those, which means we will fail for sure unless Betty Toufry can help us here. The positronic brain must have realized that we would run into telekinetic problems and that Anne Sloane would be incapable of handling them alone. Before we abandon our attempt, Betty must try to stop this robot. Come along, Betty, I'll go with you. The rest of you stay at the transmitter. And if I give the order, enter it at once. Is that clear?"

Rhodan's tone was unusually sharp. Bell decided to forego his usual argument, preferring to devote himself to the young patient lying in his arms. She was just regaining consciousness and tried to wiggle out of his firm yet tender support as soon as she became aware of this embarrassing situation.

Marshall took everything in with a certain satisfaction. Khrest was rooted to the ground as if in a trance.

Rhodan seized Betty's hand and walked back with her into the huge hall filled with machinery, in the

83

direction of the approaching robot, whose rhythmical thumping had become louder in the meantime. The monster rolled toward them with incredibly even speed.

"You must concentrate very hard," whispered Rhodan to the little girl. "It's not enough to stop the robot. Try to lift it up and carry it over to the side. You can smash it if you let it fall from a height of about five to six yards. And that is probably what they want us to do, they want us to destroy this robot. Amongst other things," he added softly as if someone might overhear him, someone who had no business listening in to his words. "Can you do it, Betty?"

The little girl nodded her head. She did not speak. Her eyes were wide open, for now they had rounded a corner and saw the metallic colossus just 10 yards in front of them. The robot rolled steadily toward them.

"Now, Betty!" whispered Rhodan. He stayed one step behind the child to avoid any unnecessary distraction.

The girl could hardly suppress the sudden panic that welled up in her. Only once in her young life had she been put to the test of proving her special abilities in an emergency situation. That time several years ago when she had to shoot her father, whose mind had been taken over by hostile alien intruders. These mind snatchers were capable of directing the bodies of other beings according to their own evil plans. The moment they had Betty's father in their power and commanded him to cause tremendous harm to all mankind, Betty had been left no other alternative but to seize her father's gun and kill him with it. Thereupon the alien invaders had been successfully repelled. However the memory of this tragic deed had caused the child to mature very rapidly.

She was a high quality mutant. Ever since she had been a small child her abilities had been fully developed. And now, at the age of nine, she surpassed all the adult mutants. Rhodan fondly characterized her as the precursor of future mankind.

Homo superior!

Betty switched off all other thoughts, concentrating exclusively on one effort to direct her mind into a beam of telekinetic energy. And then she acted with lightning speed.

Rhodan had not been able to observe how difficult it had been for Anne Sloane to lift the first robot off the ground, he had only heard the resulting crash. Nevertheless, he was amazed to watch how skillfully little Betty was "working" once she had gotten over her first shock.

The robot, which had to weigh many tons, had stopped abruptly. Its brightly illuminated eyes seemed to shine more intensely. In vain, the monster tried to push against the invisible obstacle of the telekinetic wall of energy. Its wheels spun wildly and finally stopped moving.

And then, as if it had become weightless from one moment to the next, the colossus rose upwards until its antennae bumped into the ceiling. Betty let it dangle there as if she enjoyed playing with her unusual forces.

And then she too let go suddenly.

The crashing breakup of the huge metallic body was accompanied by the terrified shouts of several people.

Rhodan whirled around in confusion. He could distinguish Bell's shrill voice and Marshall's mournful complaint. Khrest uttered a few unintelligible words.

Rhodan understood immediately that something extraordinary must have happened. He could not see what it had been because the bend in the corridor obliterated his view. He grasped Betty's arm, to lead her back to the rest of the party. It took several seconds until the child's mind returned to present time. Then she followed him willingly. Her task had been accomplished for the time being.

As Rhodan came around the bend he stopped so suddenly that Betty ran into him. Now he saw what had been the cause of his friends' commotion.

The matter transmitter that had brought them to this place and which represented their only link with the outside world, had vanished.

Sgt. Groll stood beside Lossoshér in front of the entrance to the shaft.

Both had spent a rather restless night in the narrow cabin of their fighter plane. The pilot's sleep had been constantly interrupted by the fidgety Ferronian scientist who was too excited to fall asleep. Lossoshér kept mumbling to himself, which drove Groll to distraction. He cursed the hour when Rhodan and Deringhouse had ordered him to fly the Ferronian scientist throughout the Vega system.

Finally the far distant sun rose on the horizon and the short day of moon 13B began.

They had breakfast, eating very fast and then, heavily armed, the two men returned to the plateau, the

86

scene of last night's weird encounter.

They came upon the pyramid. Groll filmed the inscription on the side of the structure. Then the two walked over to the nearby underground tunnel.

Both were gripped by fear as they peeked inside the gently descending passage. There was no light coming from within. The floor showed no joints and consisted of some concrete substance. Undoubtedly the tunnel had been constructed by some intelligent creatures.

"We have found them!" whispered Lossoshér jubilantly. "We have found those that live longer than the sun. We have outwitted them in their game of hide-and-seek. We have detected this shaft that leads down to some hiding-place. This must have been constructed by some beings that may have been dead for many years, centuries or even millennia."

"Well, what are we going to do now?" wondered Groll; "are you going down first?"

The Ferron's hair stood on end. Groll knew that this meant both fright and especially rejection. "You are my pilot," insisted Lossoshér. "You are supposed to protect me. I am nothing but a peaceful explorer. I don't know how to handle arms. You go ahead, will you!"

Sgt. Groll cursed once again that he had been entrusted with this undesirable job, but then his pride won out. Damn it, if this Ferron was going to claim later on to have been responsible for having ferreted out the unknowns' hiding-place, he wanted to be able to insist that he too had had a part in it.

He switched on the searchlight and entered the tunnel first. He had to bend over slightly. This was the first clue about the unknown builders of this shaft. They must have been shorter than Earthmen. About the size of the squat Ferron. Lossoshér would have no difficulty walking down this low-ceilinged passage.

Something did not seem right there: the stranger last night had definitely been taller than Groll himself. However Groll did not waste any time pondering about this evident inconsistency. He concentrated on the immediate task confronting him. As far as he could make out in the light of his powerful flashlight, the corridor seemed to stretch way ahead without any indication where it would end. It descended at an angle of about 20 degrees and Groll was grateful for his ribbed rubber soles that gave him a firm grip on the ground and would not let him slip or stumble. Besides, the tunnel was narrow enough that he could steady himself against the side walls with both arms stretched out.

Lossoshér followed close behind, guiding himself clumsily along the walls. The men could have advanced along the shaft with eyes closed as long as there were no side corridors.

Gradually the entrance to the world above shrank to a tiny spot of light. Even if their flashlight gave out, it would not matter greatly. They could not lose their way. Groll felt reassured.

After having advanced for about 50 yards, their searchlight was reflected by a smooth cross-wall. The material of which this wall consisted absorbed 50% of the light. What remained was bright enough to blind them.

Groll reduced the intensity of the beam. He explored the smooth wall with carefully groping fingers. The surface felt cool to his touch and somehow very massive. He rejected a thought that flitted through his mind of removing this obstacle with his hand raygun. The ensuing heat would be unbearable in this narrow passage, quite apart from the fact that the energy would most likely be insufficient to melt down this massive wall.

Anyhow, this wall proved that the unknown from the previous night must be very familiar with these surroundings—otherwise they would have come upon him by now. Unless—this thought now crossed Groll's mind—the stranger had left the tunnel again after he and Lossoshér had returned to their space fighter for the night.

"Doesn't it continue any more here?" asked Lossoshér.

"I'm sure it does," replied Groll, "behind this cross-wall."

"I wouldn't count on that with such certainty!"

The pilot did not answer. He realized that he did not possess the extensive knowledge of the Ferronian scientist, who owed this in turn to the Arkonide hypno-training he had received. Sgt. Groll had just good common sense. And this told him that this tunnel would make no sense if it ended here. There must of necessity be a continuation. Furthermore, this obstacle indicated that valuable objects probably lay hidden behind it.

He arrived therefore at the logical conclusion that this obstacle in their path had to be cleared away. Systematically he set out to accomplish this feat.

It took hardly two minutes until he found the tiny

raised bump on the right hand side of the wall at a height of approximately one yard.

He pressed in on the raised bump.

Nothing happened for a while, but then the wall started to move. It slid upward and disappeared in the slightly vaulted ceiling, which must be lying, according to his estimate, about 20 yards below the rocky surface.

At the same time bright lights flared up in front of them. He noticed that the tunnel grew wider and higher. It continued for another 10 yards and then opened into a large room which was filled with an array of glittering instruments, machines and installations.

Just before the corridor widened into the large hall, and silhouetted against the strong light coming from behind, stood a figure. Its scaly armour shimmered threateningly.

The stranger was waiting for them. Groll stared into the black mouth of a weapon that was pointed directly at him.

5 COUNTDOWN TO ETERNITY

FOR the first time in his life Perry Rhodan experienced the sensation of utter dejection. Without the matter transmitter, he realized, their way back had been cut off. It was no longer possible to escape this labyrinth of mysterious machinery. Their search for eternal life would end now in eternal death.

But this attack of despondency lasted but a few seconds. Rhodan's mind began to work again. The positronic brain could not have been wrong in its advice. And the immortals who had puzzled out this riddle would never have intended that those who were supposed to solve the riddle would perish so miserably and without any chance of extricating themselves from this precarious situation.

But where would they find the next task that was waiting to be solved?

There were thousands of tasks, according to the decoded written message. Which task was the right one, the decisive one?

And as far as the transmitter was concerned . . .

With a sudden flash of insight it became clear to Rhodan that its disappearance did not really matter. At all costs they must avoid letting themselves be confused. For this very fact itself constituted one of the tasks confronting them: don't become entrapped in confusion! And it was probably not even necessary to solve all the thousands of riddles if they should discover the decisive ones first.

"What next?" asked Khrest with a surprising calmness in his voice. "Will that mean the end for us?"

"No, Khrest. This is just the beginning." Rhodan hoped deep inside himself that he had not told a lie. "We must continue with our search."

"Now even the repair robot is no good to us," reflected Bell. "After all, how could it repair a transmitter that is no longer here?"

"There must be hidden somewhere another chance for us that will help us to return," suggested Rhodan. And this time he was convinced he was right in his assumption.

"If only we knew where we are," complained Bell. "In the interior of the planet Ferrol? On another planet? Still in the Vega system? The transmission might have hurled us to the end of the universe."

"Agreed," admitted Rhodan. "We might be anywhere or anytime. Whether on Ferrol or thousands of light years away, in the past or in the future—the way back will lead only via a matter transmitter. Therefore, we must find one, in case the old one has disappeared for good. I am afraid it has teleported itself away from here under its own power."

For the first time little Betty Toufry spoke up: "That's right. And exactly at the very same instant when the second of the hostile robots was destroyed."

Rhodan glanced at her in amazement. His thoughts began to race. Then he smiled. "Of course, we almost forgot! The moment both robots ceased to exist as functioning machines, they released a contact. The disappearance of the transmitter signifies therefore that we have come closer to our goal. It sounds paradoxical but it is a logical conclusion. Thanks, Betty. You have helped us a great deal."

"I wish I could share your optimism," said Bell, who started walking down the corridor that led between the machines. He did not even turn around when Rhodan inquired where he was going.

"I am searching for the next task, Perry."

"We must not get separated," advised Khrest. "We must stay together if we want to find the solution to this problem."

Rhodan, followed by the rest of the group, started to move in the direction Bell had taken.

"How could the positronic brain have possibly known that we would need Betty down here?" wondered Rhodan. Khrest was at a loss for an explanation too.

The passage widened. An empty pedestal with a slanting step leading up to it marked the spot where the robot had been standing. Directly above it glowed the sphere that had served as the receiving terminal for those terrifying bolts of lightning. The electrical discharges had begun after they had been scrutinized by the telepathic automaton. One event had released the next—a kind of controlled chain reaction.

Which event would now follow the disappearance of their matter transmitter?

They did not have to wait very long for an answer to their question.

Bell had been standing at the center of the widened passage. The heat was not too noticeable at this particular spot, although the entire room had become considerably warmer. There were no machines nearby.

Only a massive metal cube of about one cubic yard was over to the right. It was completely smooth, without any joints, with a strange looking instrument resting on top.

There was hardly enough time for Rhodan to examine this instrument properly. He mainly noticed various levers, sliding scales and buttons. The mysterious apparatus reminded him remotely of a movie camera. An oval-shaped lens confirmed this impression.

A gentle humming roar came from somewhere again.

Suddenly Bell started to shriek in horror without any visible cause; he kept screaming at the top of his voice. He shouted incomprehensible words, all the while raising his arms as if he were trying to grasp something invisible.

Rhodan, startled, stopped abruptly. "What's the matter?" he called out to his friend. "Did you get caught inside an energy field? I can't see anything . . ."

But now all could plainly perceive it. A nebulous veil coming from nowhere formed around Bell, whirled aimlessly around the human shape, gradually condensing to a spiral, which began systematically to envelop his body. The spiral kept turning faster and faster apparently materializing into a compact mass. Bell's figure became hazy but his disconcerted cries passed unhindered through the strange barrier.

"Stand still, Reg!" ordered Rhodan. "Is it painful?"

"I don't feel anything at all!" roared Bell in desperation. "That damn thing won't let go of me! Get me out of here! Quick!"

"Don't get hysterical! It doesn't hurt—so it can't be that dangerous."

Rhodan's thoughts were racing. There must be some reason for this energy spiral. It meant to draw his attention to something. But there was nothing in the immediate vicinity.

Oh, yes, there was something indeed!

The "movie camera"!

Rhodan jumped over to the metal cube. The lens of the strange camera—or whatever else it might be— stared at him with an almost challenging look.

And then, rising to the surface from some unfathomable depth, an almost forgotten memory emerged. Or was it just his imagination? Somewhere, sometime, he had encountered this instrument before. If not in reality, then at least in the form of a hypothetical plan.

It must have been during his hypno-training! The special schooling that had transferred to his mind the entire body of Arkonide knowledge. If this memory should stem from this training, then Khrest ought to know about it too. And most likely in more detail.

Rhodan turned to the Arkonide scientist. "Khrest! Think fast! What is this thing? I remember it vaguely from the scientific theories of the hypno-training. It was called fictional . . . no, fictive . . . oh, hell, help me, Khrest! It has something to do with dematerialization. Fifth dimensional. The Arkonides know of it only in theory. Please, think hard! Everything depends on it!"

Before Khrest had a chance to reply, Betty interjected: "It's much faster to think than to speak. Khrest has understood your question, Rhodan. This apparatus is a *fictive*-transmitter, described by the Arkonides as a theoretical possibility but never practically explored.

It functions according to the principle of fifth-dimensional geometry. Mechanical teleportation with ray impulses capable of seizing objects. This way it is possible to teleport things from any place in the universe to somewhere else."

Khrest remained silent. There was nothing he could add after little Betty had expressed all his thoughts aloud. Rhodan felt relieved. His brain worked at top speed.

Meanwhile Bell had stopped screaming. He stood motionless in the center of the wildly rotating energy spiral. He was waiting for a miracle that would free him from this imprisonment. His feet were hovering about five inches above the floor, Rhodan noted with scientific detachment. Thus he must have been removed from the fetters of gravitational pull.

Without much thought, acting more on an impulse, Rhodan's fist slammed hard on a lever that suddenly glimmered faintly on the side of the so-called camera. This time the unknowns had given him a definite hint! Perhaps this problem had seemed too difficult even to them.

At first, a strange thing happened: the camera swung around. The lens was now pointing at Bell, who followed the whole procedure with wide open eyes, although he could probably not see too much of what was going on. The shimmering veils of the energy spiral that kept dancing madly around him must of necessity partially obscure his view.

A button lit up with a red glow. At the same time the lens had completed its turn. Rhodan did not hesitate and pushed the button in. A humming sound came from the metal cube. Rhodan could feel the floor vibrate underneath his feet.

Bell cried out. He contorted his body, trying to free himself from the horrible grasp of these fetters without substance. But in vain. Betty stood stock still, listening for something from inside. She seemed to wait for a voice that would not come.

And then the wild dance of the spiral diminished. The nebulous structure grew less dense, became more transparent and weaker. It vanished completely within one second.

Bell dropped down five inches to the ground. His knees gave way under him. He looked as white as a sheet, his face painfully contorted. His red stubbly hair stood on end. It seemed to quiver with excitement. His pale lips, that had remained mute for the past few moments, formed one word only. It was not a pleasant word, but it expressed exactly what he felt. And it was not gratitude he should really have experienced now.

Yet the spooky show was not over.

Hardly had Bell's feet landed on the floor, and Rhodan breathed a sigh of relief, then the chain reaction of events continued its course.

Behind Bell was the back wall of the machine hall. This wall was smooth and without any partitions. Now this wall began to dissolve.

The wall appeared to be made of metal. It seemed to be quite thick.

The wall lost its color and began to look milky. It started to flow, to become liquefied, then the orignally solid matter began to evaporate. Now it reminded the startled onlookers of the gaseous energy spiral. All of a sudden it disappeared.

The hall had doubled in size. Before the eyes of the perplexed group lay the continuation of the secret, namely that part of the room that so far had been hidden from them.

At first glance there did not seem much difference between the two halls. But then Rhodan remarked that it contained far less machinery. At the center of the various pedestals and metal cubes, the rounded-off housings and spiral-formed pillars, stood a giant sphere. Its small delicate legs rested on a rectangular, massive platform. At first glance it resembled a miniaturized *Stardust*, for its diameter was barely 15 feet; but here, inside this hall, it loomed gigantic.

Actually, it was not a perfect sphere as Rhodan found out on closer inspection. It had numerous projections and indentations. Irregularities in the form of antennae which were sticking out and other extensions. And then Rhodan noticed something which seemed familiar: at the front end of a sizable metal rod he saw a large oval-shaped lens which played in a thousand colors and which apparently looked directly at him.

"A fictive-transmitter," he murmured slowly. Khrest nodded in silent agreement. The others did not speak. No one moved. Bell looked quite green around his gills. Anne Sloane had recovered her strength meanwhile and she grasped Betty's hand. John Marshall kept staring at the sphere, his eyes half-way closed.

Only the Arkonide robot remained totally uninvolved and stood behind the group, waiting for orders that never came. Haggard was next to it.

Rhodan walked ahead. He was the first to cross the

place where seconds earlier a solid metal wall had barred their way. The wall's matter had simply been removed by the small transmitter.

Was this another clue?

Rhodan was certain of it. He also realized that they were expected to regard this disappearing trick not as a warning but as an invitation.

Not until John Marshall and Betty Toufry stepped across the invisible barrier did the next link in the chain of events become automatically evident. Both telepathic mutants stopped suddenly. Anne let go at once of little Betty's hand.

Khrest put his hand on Rhodan's arm. Both men understood immediately that the two telepaths were receiving a new message, that neither of the non-telepaths could hear nor fathom.

Suddenly the little girl looked up at Marshall. "You have got the message, haven't you? Why don't you tell them!"

The Australian wiped both his eyes with the back of his right hand, as if he were trying to shoo away something. Then he spoke with emphasis:

"This is a further communication. Listen to this: 'You have exactly 15 minutes (according to your measure of time) in which to leave this place. However, you will find the light only if you will be able to return.' That was all. Nothing else was said. It was a telepathic suggestive voice that transmitted this message."

"Only if we shall be able to return," whispered Rhodan in a halting voice while his searching glance rested on the big sphere. The fictive-transmitter! "And we have only 15 minutes?"

"Fourteen by now!" These were Bell's first words since the incident with the energy spiral. "This could turn into a nice mess."

It became even worse than that!

From somewhere in the background came an at first hardly perceptible humming noise that soon changed to rhythmic vibrations which rapidly intensified to an unbearable ringing in their ears. They had to shout to make themselves understood. At the same time dazzling bolts of lightning flashed across the room, filling the air with a strong odour of ozone and steadily rising heat. The air grew very oppressive.

A gong sounded repeatedly at regular intervals, seemingly counting the speeding seconds. "Only 12 minutes left," said Khrest softly; but nobody could hear his words. The noise drowned out his voice.

Haggard had remained in the background all the time in such an inobtrusive manner that Rhodan almost forgot that the physician was part of the expedition. He had hardly noticed when he had administered medical aid to Anne Sloane. But now, as the group fell victim to an unbearable tension that threatened to make them lose their self-control, he intervened. He was not only a physician but also an excellent psychologist.

"No reason to get all excited!" he shouted into Rhodan's ear. And on seeing Rhodan's bitter smile he added: "They only want to test us! Our physical power of resistance! A war of nerves! The heirs to immortality must be both the vessels of superior wisdom and knowledge and also demonstrate tremendous physical stamina. Nothing but diversionary tactics on their part."

"Do you really think so?" yelled Rhodan in reply.

"I am positive! Just concentrate on searching for a chance to be able to return. Don't pay attention to the noise or the lightning flashes. The heat will grow intolerable only after the 15 minutes have gone by. And then . . ."

"Ten minutes to go!" yelled Marshall at the top of his voice. He had followed the conversation by listening in to their thoughts, since it was impossible to hear above the noise from where he stood. "We'd better hurry up!"

Rhodan did not answer. He had stepped closer to the sphere, recognizing it as an approximate enlargement of the apparatus in the other part of the hall where he had used it to remove the energy spiral and the wall. The first application had been a hint, nothing else. He had to make use of this clue in order to effect here a similar procedure. But what was supposed to be teleported from this section of the room?

The answer came with a sudden flash of insight: he and his group!

There was no opening on the giant fictive-transmitter. The sphere appeared to be solid, or perhaps filled with many instruments. There was no hollow space they could enter. This fictive-transmitter teleported via the fifth-dimensional ray impulses capable of seizing objects.

There was only one button on the instrument that might activatd it. This large button was located in plain view on the platform. It was slightly recessed and glowed red.

A wave of suspicion flooded Rhodan's mind. The solution seemed too obvious, too simple. Just walk over and depress the botton. He felt intuitively that this button would return him and the others—but where to? On the other hand his analytical mind told him that this degree of difficulty was not of the same level as those problems of the Galactic Riddle they had encountered before.

Where was the barrier?

"Eight more minutes!" warned Marshall.

It had grown much hotter in the meantime. The lightning kept flashing across the hall just above their heads, emitting explosions. The ringing of the gong swelled to a mighty roar, recurring at increasingly shorter intervals. Somewhere in the distance they began to hear once again the by now familiar thumping of an approaching robot.

Seven minutes to go!

Rhodan came to a decision. He had nothing to lose; he could only win.

"Stay here!" he shouted, trying to overcome the noise. "The ray impulses might grasp everything inside this hall—or maybe only all organic matter. I don't know. This button here . . ."

All of a sudden he became aware of something he had not noticed until now. Perhaps it had made its appearance just this very moment.

The red button was still glowing. But Rhodan thought it had begun to flicker. Just as if an invisible glass bell had formed around it.

"Damn it!" It was Bell. "Exactly five more minutes. If we don't get a move on . . ."

Rhodan could guess Bell's feelings about their desperate situation by reading his lips. He dared not waste another second. He stepped over to the sphere. The platform reached up to his chest. The recessed red button lay directly below Rhodan's exploring glance. His body was hiding the light sources and the bright lightning bolts. The glass bell had disappeared.

He jerked into action. His hand reached for the button while his forehead beaded with perspiration. The next second would decide the fate of his entire group. Either they would return to Thorta or they would be condemned to perish in this hell of the unleashed power of robots gone berserk.

Rhodan's hand was barely two inches away from the button when he encountered a smooth, cool, invisible barrier. It felt like glass but Rhodan knew that this was no ordinary glass. This strange substance was vibrating and seemed alive. It sent out a weak current which passed through Rhodan's entire body.

He could not get to the botton.

"Three more minutes!"

Bell was screaming so loud that his voice drowned out the roaring gong. For the first time, Rhodan thought, Bell's words contained a genuine note of desperation and helplessness. They had squandered their last chance.

Just two inches separated them from the button that might save them—but it was out of reach. An impenetrable wall of pure yet neutralized energy formed an impenetrable barrier. No hand could pass through this obstacle.

The heat had become extremely oppressive. The air was suffocating; it was hard to breathe. Little Betty was panting, gasping for oxygen. The clatter of the approaching death-dealing robot sounded louder and more foreboding. Doom came nearer in many forms.

"Oh damn it!" Bell screamed again. "Ninety seconds to go!"

Ninety seconds to eternity. And they had set out searching for eternal life. Now there was only sudden death awaiting them. Had they reached their goal?

All of a sudden the lightning ceased. They could still hear the sound of the gong but quite soft and muffled. The vibrations of the approaching robot grew still.

And then all could hear an inaudible voice, which spoke to them. This voice came from the void and formed thought concepts inside their brains. Was this the way telepaths received their messages? But this time not only the two telepaths but all of them could understand:

"You have just a few more moments left! Apply the ultimate wisdom and knowledge—otherwise you will be lost forever . . ."

Hardly had the entire message come through than Rhodan called out with extreme agitation:

"Betty! The red button! Push it down, quick!"

The little girl understood at once. No human hand was capable of reaching that button. But if light rays could penetrate the energy barrier then telepathic thought currents of the "upper order" could do likewise.

And as Bell was calling out with dwindling hope "only 30 more seconds left!" Betty bore down on the red button with all the concentration and strength she could muster.

Rhodan saw it quite clearly. The button sank in its frame as if moved by a ghostly hand. And simultaneously, contacts were made in the interior of the gigantic sphere, currents of energy began to flow, passing through transformers, then the currents were conducted into the fourth and then fifth dimension; the mechanism started turning the crystal lens around until it pointed directly at the assembled group of desperate people. The entire complicated and so far incomprehensible procedure had been set in motion and could no longer be stopped.

And then, as the last few remaining seconds fled by, the bolts of lightning resumed. The gong resumed its roar. The thundering, rhythmical robot began to move ahead, thumping threateningly. The temperature rose rapidly and became insupportable during the final moments.

The last traces of remaining oxygen in the air were entirely used up.

But now—and everyone felt it—the characteristic gnawing pain coursed through their limbs. Everything began to grow hazy in front of their eyes; the sphere changed to a pleasant Nirvana.

They dematerialized and were hurtled through the fifth dimension. They were unaware that the giant machine hall with the fictive-transmitter inside became vapourized in the sudden hell of an atomic chain reaction.

WHILE Sgt. Groll stared into the muzzle of a strange weapon, the seconds seemed to stretch into an eternity.

He no longer paid heed to Lossoshér who was standing behind him. He saw only the figure that had now become a threatening shadow—the unknown enemy and guardian of the labyrinth.

The foe hesitated. And this was his downfall.

The Ferron's eyes had adjusted faster to the sudden brightness than was possible for the Earthman. While Groll's eyes could take in merely the weapon, Lossoshér already perceived a great deal more.

"It's a Topide!" he hissed excitedly. "Shoot him! Quick!"

With these words he dropped to the ground.

Later on, Groll would never have been able to tell how rapidly the raygun—which he had stashed away in his belt again—had snapped back into his hand once more, ready to blast away. The mere mention of the word "Topide" had sufficed to make him react instinctively and lightning fast. Thus the creature which had been an unknown quantity so far had instantly changed into a deadly foe.

The Topides! They were the lizard-like intelligent race that had come here from a solar system over 800 light-years distant because they had intercepted the distress signals emitted years ago by an Arkonide research space cruiser which had crash-landed on

Earth's celestial satellite. The Topides, however, had miscalculated the space coordinates and arrived instead in the Vega system, where they encountered bitter resistance from the native Ferrons. Not until Perry Rhodan intervened in the fight had the alien invaders been driven out.

What a surprise to meet up with a hostile reptilian Topide here on the outermost moon of the 13th planet!

These thoughts raced through Groll's mind as he threw himself to the ground. Just before he hit the floor he managed to push down the firing button. He saw the fiery energy beam rush toward the shadowy figure of the enemy at the same moment Groll's blinded eyes closed in a reflex action.

But the Topide had also recognized the dangerous situation. For some inexplicable reason he had hesitated—far too long. This was fortunate for Groll and Lossoshér—they owed their lives to this tiny delay.

The Topide had opened fire at the same time as Groll. But the lizard creature had been too slow in his reactions. While the Terran aimed at a relatively immobile figure, the Topide, on the other hand, shot at an opponent who was no longer there. The energy rays of his weapon raced just above the two men, now pressed to the ground, safe from the searing ray of destruction.

Meanwhile the deadly beam from Groll's gun executed a mad, fiery dance macabre. Then all went dark.

Groll opened his eyes. The big shadow had vanished but on the spot where it had stood there now glowed a dustlike substance giving off billowing clouds of smoke. The lights of the room beyond glimmered weakly but this was just an optical illusion due to the aftereffect of the dazzling energy flashes. It would take a little while before their eyes would get used again to normal conditions.

Lossoshér stirred and then sat up. "A Topide! What's a Topide doing here?"

Groll was the last person who could enlighten him on this subject. As far as he knew the alien invaders had been driven out of the Vega system.

"Maybe a survivor of the space battles who managed to flee here. In that case we should find his lifeboat somewhere around. Perhaps that's why he hesitated. Who knows, he might have hoped we had come to his rescue."

The Ferron stood up, then helped Groll to his feet.

"I wonder if he was the only one here?"

Groll knew no answer to that question either. In any case, he made sure to keep the raygun in his hand while they proceeded toward the end of the corridor. They advanced another 10 yards. Then both men stood before a technological miracle beyond their understanding.

One of the walls of the long, low-ceilinged room was covered by a row of opalescent picture-screens. Six-feet-tall transistors alternated with weighty blocks of a copper-coloured metal, all conjoined by silvery shimmering connecting rods. In between were black spheres with pointed antennae. The wall at the opposite end consisted of a gigantic switchboard. The maze of levers, buttons and control lamps heightened the confusion.

"What is that?" Groll was dumbfounded. He had expected something quite different, although he could not tell exactly what. Lossoshér was none too sure himself, nevertheless he said: "A technical installation of the immortals, what else!"

Groll kept staring a few more moments at the collection of all these mystifying instruments and installations. Then he made up his mind. "We must return to Ferrol immediately and inform Rhodan about what happened here and what we have found. Only he and the Arkonides are capable of comprehending the purpose of this room. Let's leave, Lossoshér; every second counts now."

The Ferronian scientist had gone ahead meanwhile. He stopped in front of the first picture-screen. He searched in vain for the control buttons.

"Leave everything alone!" Groll's voice sounded harsh and commanding. "Don't tamper with things you don't understand! You might cause untold trouble if you start messing around with instruments of an unknown supertechnology. Come along! We have no time to waste!"

The Ferronian scientist could tear himself away only very reluctantly from the marvels of an incomprehensible past. For there was no doubt in his mind that this installation was far older than his own nation's first attempts at space travel.

"I'm certain this is what Rhodan has been looking for." Then he turned around. "You are right, Sergeant. Let's go!"

As soon as they again reached the cross-wall, now only recognizable by a very low threshold, the lights behind them went out. Once more the entire hall lay in darkness. Groll whipped out his flashlight and switched it on. The sudden darkness seemed oppressive.

Barely 10 seconds after the lights had gone out, the wall that had separated the two sections of the huge room descended once more from the ceiling to the floor. It was slowly gliding down, shutting off the installation from the outside world.

Without a word, the two men walked back the same way they had entered a while earlier. Far ahead they could see daylight in the form of a tiny oval opening. Soon they came out into the bright light of the Vega sun.

Groll suddenly began to shiver. His warm overalls could not keep out the cold. He realized that this icy feeling which gripped his body was not due to any cold outside temperature. It seemed to him that he had killed a living being barely a few seconds ago, although the incident with the Topide must have happened more than half an hour earlier. Suddenly he was filled with doubt. Had he done the right thing? What if the Topide had been shipwrecked on this strange moon? He should have been entitled to any assistance they could have offered him according to the interstellar code.

He quickly rejected these thoughts. After all, the Topide had died with a drawn weapon in his hand.

Lossoshér had walked a few steps over to the side and stopped in front of the pyramid. With half-closed eyes, straining to see, he stared at the inscription. The resemblance to the symbols that Rhodan had deciphered with the help of the positronic brain was quite obvious.

"Here is your proof, Sergeant, that we are on the right track. We have discovered what we came to find.

It's all right with me if we start at once and fly back to Ferrol."

Groll did not reply. He could very well understand Lossoshér's enthusiastic feelings. But why, he wondered, didn't he share his joy? He ought to have been so happy to have done something to please Rhodan.

Let's wait and see, he thought to himself, what this inscription is all about. They had made snapshots and the instantly developed pictures were safely stashed inside Lossoshér's pocket.

Silently, the two returned to the waiting space figher. The lock was exactly the way they had left it. They climbed into the narrow cockpit. Ten seconds later the rocky landscape of the plateau fell away below them.

"Look! Down there!" Lossoshér suddenly called out in amazement. "Over there, near that rock, something is glittering in the sun . . ." Now they were directly above it. They recognized the bent and twisted remnants of a tiny space vessel, a kind of lifeboat used to find a haven of refuge within this system by those unfortunate space travelers whose ship had been wrecked.

"That means there was only one of them here on this moon," Groll said quietly. He continued thinking to himself: He was the last Topide in this system. And I have killed him.

He pushed the joystick forward. The racy fighter plane shot up into the suddenly darkening sky.

Darkness!

Occasional whirlpools of glittering colours, flashing lights. Gnawing pains in all limbs. Endless falling into infinite space. Ghastly loneliness in eternity. Neither cold nor heat—total nothingness.

Only one thing—consciousness, awareness!

Time? It had lost any significance, had turned into absolute abstractness. Seconds . . . years . . . millions of years——

Distance? It no longer existed. Miles . . . light-years . . . billions of light-years——

And suddenly the present returned!

Rhodan felt the gnawing pain leave him. The wide open eyes could see again. His feet felt firm ground underneath. He had a body once more.

And he could hear again. Namely Bell's hoarse voice.

"We made it! The vault! Perry, we are back in the crypt!"

Now Rhodan could see it too.

Through the wire fence of the well-known transmitter he recognized the underground hall on Thorta. Three of his four mutants were standing close to the entrance. Their faces showed an unmistakable expression of utter consternation.

Unconsciously, Rhodan looked at his watch.

They had spent four hours altogether in that mysterious machine hall.

It had seemed like an eternity to him.

He pushed—and the door of the transmitter sprang open.

The African Ras Tschubai walked toward Rhodan, who was the first to leave the wire cage.

"Back so soon, sir?"

Rhodan felt perplexed. "Soon? What is that supposed to mean, Ras?"

"You were hardly gone, just five minutes, sir."

Rhodan peered into the African's eyes. He tried to hide his surprise. He said calmly: "Let's compare our watches, Ras."

The teleporter glanced at his wristwatch. "Exactly 10:30 Terran standard time, sir."

Rhodan slowly lifted his arm. He looked at his chronometer. Just what he had thought. The hands pointed to 14:25 o'clock.

"You had hardly left when the robot reappeared. He teleported himself back to the base via matter transmitter and returned within three or four minutes with little Betty. He has hardly come back to the crypt again. Less than a minute."

Meanwhile the others had stepped out of the matter transmitter. Only Khrest understood what Ras was talking about. What was wrong? What had happened to the time? They had lived physically through four hours—within less than five minutes.

A whiff, a presentiment of eternity?

Anne Sloane's scream rent the air. She had been the last person to leave the transmitter cage, just behind Marshall. Quite by accident she had looked up at the ceiling. And now she saw it.

Whoever did not see it, could hear it.

Up above, close to the ceiling, floated a small glowing sphere. Its diameter could not be more than four inches. It pulsated slowly and rhythmically. The regular contractions were accompanied by muffled hollow-sounding gong beats, identical to those heard in the machine hall they had just left.

Rhodan whirled around when Anne's voice rang out. He saw the sphere and his body stiffened.

The light?

The message had spoken of a light they could not find until they returned. All right, they had returned now. This glowing sphere must be the light! But what was it all supposed to mean?

The sphere radiated as intensely as if it were a glowing ball of fire. Then, with infinite slowness, it began to sink lower. Rhodan knew instinctively that there must be some time limit to this phenomenon. The unknowns had so far adhered to the principle that the solution of a task must always be accomplished within a certain limited time.

Bell's hair looked all disheveled. The glow of the radiant sphere was reflected from his red, bristling crewcut. For a moment his head seemed to be on fire. Rhodan glanced in fascination for an instant at this strange spectacle. Then he turned to Betty. "Can you hear anything? Any telepathic message? Marshall, how about you?"

The two mutants shook their heads. The sphere remained mute.

Khrest stared at the glowing sphere. "It consists of pure energy, no doubt. But I don't believe that it is existing in the here and now. It is glowing but it does not radiate any heat. Cold light."

Bell was forced to step to the side. The sphere had continued to descend and had almost landed on his head. Still those muffled, mysterious gong beats! Everyone without exception had their eyes glued to the strange ball of light. A new task to solve! It seemed to have brought along with it the horrors of the machine hall they had barely escaped.

Rhodan addressed himself to Anne Sloane. "Can you stop the sphere or direct its course, Anne?"

The young girl tried but her telekinetic powers deserted her. The sphere simply continued on its downward course, pulsating mysteriously, constantly issuing the soft, monotonous gong beats. They sounded like precious seconds falling into the ocean of eternity.

Now the sphere was floating close to Bell's face. He no longer attempted to avoid it. His eyes were almost closed in order to be able to bear the mild glow. Now the glowing ball was barely eight inches away from his face. He felt no warmth.

Instead he could see something.

Perhaps it was the sphere's proximity that permitted him to see the dark, elongated object inside the ball. The object resembled a single cell as seen under an electron microscope—a transparent round mass with a dark spot at its center, no longer than two inches.

Before Rhodan or anyone else could judge what Bell was about to do, the stocky redhead had already started to act. Throwing all caution aside, Bell resolutely stuck his hand inside the sphere, trying to grasp the dark object. He was convinced he had found the long awaited message.

His thought processes were not devoid of logic. They had been promised the light. This sphere was condensed, cold light. At its center was a dark object which could only be a capsule. Containing the message. The next task.

His deliberations were rudely interrupted.

Hardly had his fingertips touched the periphery of the light ball, when it gave off short, colorful flashes of lightning which disappeared in Bell's hand. Simultaneously—Rhodan noticed this with consternation and amazement—Bell's hair began to shine brightly. His stiff bristles stood on edge, changing into a polar light display.

Bell's horrified screams led the others to believe that he did not particularly appreciate such use of his head of hair. With a sharp jerky movement he withdrew his hand from the fiery ball, then started to dance around the vault like a wild Indian, all the while shaking his arms, trying to get rid of all electrical currents coursing through his body.

In the meantime the sphere continually sank lower and lower. Now it hovered barely five feet above the ground. What a catastrophe, thought Rhodan, if it reaches the floor. Who knows what calamity might befall us! At best, the sphere will simply vanish into the ground and be lost forever. And with it, the dark capsule, which he had also seen meanwhile, and which Reg had tried to retrieve in vain.

Now Betty Toufry took over from Anne Sloane who had endeavoured to stop the sphere's steady descent by means of telekinesis. Little Betty concentrated her efforts on the capsule. She assumed that it was staying in present time and in three-dimensional space. Unfortunately, it soon became evident that little Betty's efforts also were unsuccessful. Nothing seemed capable of stemming the ball's unflagging downward progress.

Bell had calmed down somewhat. Now he regarded the light-ball like a personal enemy.

"It scared the hell out of me," he confided. "At first it had seemed rather friendly and peaceful."

Rhodan looked at him with growing interest. "What do you mean by that? Peaceful?"

"Yes, Perry. Peaceful. The electrical jolts did not come until later. In the beginning a very gentle current flowed from the sphere into my fingers, coursed through my body and then returned to the sphere. That's when the fireworks started! It did not hurt too much. I could have gotten used to it in time."

Rhodan's eyes followed pensively the descending ball that was now barely three feet above the floor. "Sounds almost as if the ball was examining you. Maybe it did not like what it found!"

"Maybe you will pass this inspection, Perry. It might grow fond of you." Bell sounded annoyed but soon his sarcasm gave way to a more rational approach. He glanced at his friend, then to the sphere, finally fixed his eyes on Rhodan. "If we both think the same, then it's high time you started to act . . ."

Rhodan briefly nodded his assent.

The risk could not be too great, for Reg had survived the contact with the fiery sphere. The unknowns who had sent them this ball of cold light were not malicious after all. They just had a strange sense of humor. Though they played dangerous games with the lives of their potential successors, they never presented a direct and inescapable threat to their survival.

If Bell had come through this ordeal unscathed, without any harmful aftereffects, then he himself should not fare any worse. Particularly since he had been forewarned. On the other hand, there was Bell's description of the probing electrical fingers. That was a definite clue he ought not overlook. Who knew, Reg might have been right in guessing that he lacked the proper thought structure.

The sphere hovered one foot above the floor. Rhodan bent over and resolutely reached into the light-ball.

At once he felt the gentle ripplings of the weak currents of energy that flooded through his body. But there were no flashes of lightning. Bell noticed this with a mixture of annoyance and gratification.

The light was indeed cold, stated Rhodan. The initial ripples soon ceased; no feeling, no sensation of any electrical currents remained.

But his fingertips encountered something hard and substantial. The capsule was undoubtedly of a three-dimensional nature.

Rhodan grasped it easily between his thumb and index finger. It felt cold to the touch, but not too cold. Gently he pulled it out from inside the sphere.

It was a metal capsule, two inches long and half an inch thick. One side was covered by a lid. Inside this capsule, however, Rhodan felt positive he would find the message of light.

He breathed deeply and stepped aside. Now that he held the capsule in his hands, his calmness and poise returned. And his analytical mind as well.

"We'd better leave the vault now," he said to his group. "Let's watch from the entrance what will happen to the sphere once it reaches the floor."

The gong beats had ceased. This was the only noticeable change. The sphere was still glowing brightly, sinking steadily, finally touching the smooth rocky ground of the vault. Meanwhile, Rhodan and his friends had retreated to the entrance of the huge subterranean hall. They were watching, observing, full of suspense, anxiously awaiting the next events.

The sphere touched the ground—and sank down into it.

As if there were nothing obstructing its path, it kept steadily penetrating the solid rock. Now it could be seen, a glowing hemisphere resting on the stone, growing smaller and smaller. Just like the setting sun dipping and disappearing into the ocean.

Finally the last glow vanished. The sphere was gone.

"Fantastic!" Khrest exclaimed; he was obviously most impressed by the spectacle he had just witnessed. "It has returned into its own dimension. If you had not pulled out this capsule, it would have disappeared now together with the light-ball."

"Yes, Khrest. And with it the solution of the Galactic Riddle—or at least, a part of the puzzle that we are supposed to figure out."

"You mean there is more to come? More problems?"

Rhodan shrugged his shoulders. "Perhaps we will get an answer to that from the positronic brain. Let's go!"

As the group was leaving the vault, Rhodan switched off the generator that had maintained the vault within present time. The machine's soft hum died down. The matter transmitter and metal boxes vanished as if they had never existed.

Nothing remained but the empty, deserted underground crypt.

7   MENTAL GIANTS

THE gigantic spacesphere *Stardust* looked almost tiny as it rested below the iridescent dome of energy. The Arkonide battleship had a diameter of over 800 yards. Inside its giant hangars it harboured among many other things two entire squadrons of the faster-than-light space fighters. A crew of 300 manned the monstrous structure whose control center represented a miracle of non-human technology. Perry Rhodan and Reginald Bell understood this technology only thanks to the Arkonide hypno-training. Within a few days they had been schooled in the age-old wisdom and knowledge that was the exclusive heritage of the ruling race of the universe.

Rhodan still marveled at the ship's propulsion drive that permitted the *Stardust* to jump across distances of many light-years during the course of a few moments. Yet he was even more impressed by the mighty positronic brain. In it he saw the crowning achievement of the Arkonides' inventive genius. The memory banks of the positronic brain held the entire body of knowledge that the superior Arkonide intellect had accumulated. But whereas the Arkonide race underwent a process of degeneration, the brain could never fall victim to this gradual decay. On the contrary, the creation had already far surpassed its creators.

This fact was the only potential danger it might represent.

Perry Rhodan knew that the positronic brain's intricate installations were hidden behind the heavy walls of Arkonite, a metal alloy capable of lasting for millions of years. Rhodan had never seen the interior of the brain. He was familiar only with the exterior mechanisms of switches and keyboards. The face of the highest intellect of the universe consisted of an array of levers, buttons, switches, dials and loudspeakers.

It had been easy for Rhodan to open the capsule he had taken from the glowing sphere. Inside he found a rolled-up sheaf made of some unknown material. It was covered with symbols that were illuminated from within. Some of these symbols looked familiar but most were strange and mysterious.

The positronic brain had been working for over five hours already trying to decipher the cryptic inscription. Hours full of waiting, hope and nerve-racking despair.

Finally the answer came. It was most disappointing.

"The message is encoded. It is being passed onto a special section. It will take an indefinite number of days before any real result can be expected."

Khrest, Thora and Bell had just entered the center and heard the mechanical voice of the brain as it communicated its provisional findings.

"Damn it!" Bell growled. "No solution! Just another mystery."

Thora's reaction to the answer was a furious outbreak. "Perry, as far as I am concerned, the planet of eternal life does not exist at all! We are chasing a trail that was a reality thousands of years ago. Today it leads us merely a merry chase that endangers our lives. And if indeed an immortal race does exist, we could find it much easier with more conventional means."

Rhodan turned around slowly. "And what might these more conventional means be, Thora?"

"Spaceflights! This is what this fabulous ship has been intended for originally. On our way back to Arkon we will approach each of the systems and examine them for inhabited planets."

"You are forgetting two things, Thora," Rhodan interrupted. "First of all, between here and the planet Arkon lies a distance of some 34,000 light-years, filled with more solar systems than you could ever explore. Secondly, the planet of eternal life—if it ever did exist—is supposed to have been located here in the Vega system. This planet has migrated to some unknown place. It could be anywhere in the universe. What guarantee do you have that it took off in the direction of your home planet Arkon? It could just as well have taken the opposite direction. We don't even know its speed. Perhaps it still continues to wander, a planet without a sun, rushing through the universe. A restless, immortal wanderer. No, Thora, your proposition is unacceptable."

"Why don't you suggest a better one!" Thora challenged him furiously. "But make it a good one, please. Otherwise we will have to wait a very long time before you bring us back to Arkon."

"I understand, Thora." Rhodan's voice sounded suddenly very weary. "That is your main concern: Arkon! I promise you will see your home planet again as soon as we have solved the Galactic Riddle and have found the planet of eternal life."

Thora turned away abruptly. Her beautiful face became a rigid, hostile mask. Khrest noticed this change with dismay. He tried to reconcile the two opposing views. "You must show some understanding for Thora, Perry. Our scientific council ordered her to explore this sector of the galaxy. Only because of our unforeseen crash-landing on Terra's moon have you had the opportunity to take possession of our technology and our knowledge. It is true, we permitted it, and even helped you with this, as we hoped this would enable us to return to our home some day. But now, our goal is being pushed farther and farther ahead into the future."

"Didn't your expedition set out on a search for the planet of eternal life?"

"Yes, but . . ."

"But that is exactly what I am trying to accomplish! We are both working toward one common goal. I can't understand Thora's attitude."

"Just consider, Perry." Khrest began anew but was abruptly interrupted. A red light bulb lit up in front of Rhodan, who automatically flipped the switch of the intercom. Maj. Deringhouse's face appeared on the visiscreen.

"Yes, Deringhouse, what is it?"

"My pilot Sgt. Groll had just reported back from his mission with Lossoshér, the Ferronian scientist. Lossoshér urgently wants to talk to you. He claims to have found the planet of eternal life."

Utter silence reigned for a few moments in the control room. The news came like a shock for everyone. Thora breathed hard, while Khrest managed to hide his feelings behind an exterior mask of indifference.

Bell's mouth was wide open; he was overwhelmed by the announcement. Rhodan commanded: "Have Groll and Lossoshér report here immediately."

The Ferron soon arrived and with a triumphant gesture he handed Rhodan the photos he had taken of the pyramid. Groll stood next to him. It was obvious that he felt ill at ease.

"We found the pyramid on the second moon of the 13th planet," Lossoshér said, "close to a shaft that led deep inside a rocky plateau. We entered this underground tunnel and penetrated deep below the surface where we discovered highly complex technical installations. It was the general belief of our scientists that this moon was uninhabited and had always been so. It still appears this way. These installations seem to be the remnants of a dead civilization. On the other hand it could just as well be that energy centre which tore the former 10th planet of our solar system out of its established orbit around the Vega sun and changed the planet to one of the moons of the 13th planet. If this theory should prove to be true then 13B would be none other than the planet of eternal life."

Rhodan had listened intently to Lossoshér's report. He held the photo in his hand, glancing at it repeatedly as if he could not decide what to do with it. Finally he inserted it quickly into the proper slot of the positronic brain. He pushed a button and set an extremely involved procedure in motion. Optical lenses focused on the inscription, reproduced the symbols in electronic impulses which were sped on their way instantaneously. Thus the process of decoding was set in motion.

Rhodan glanced at Lossoshér. "Did you find any trace of life on this moon?"

"Yes, just a Topidian lizard. Sgt. Groll shot him."

"A Topide? How is that possible?"

Groll spoke up. "Probably a survivor of the recent invading forces. He must have escaped from the holocaust of our space battles. His lifeboat was severely damaged when he crash-landed on the 13th moon. He must also have discovered the underground tunnel. In any case he awaited us there when we descended into the shaft."

"And you killed a defenseless person in distress?" Rhodan blamed the sergeant. "You know very well that such an action is punishable according to the laws of the Third Power—according to all interstellar conventions."

"I acted in self-defense. The Topide pointed his gun at me. My aim was better and faster. So he was killed instead of me."

Lossoshér came to his rescue. "It happened exactly the way Sgt. Groll has told you. He was only doing his duty. He defended our lives when we were both attacked and in danger of being destroyed."

Crackling sounds came from the loudspeaker near the ceiling. The acoustics of the positronic brain were warming up. Then the mechanical, soulless voice announced: "Translation completed. The result will be in form of a written report. End of message."

Rhodan turned to Khrest. "That was fast. Faster than I expected. The inscription was probably not even written in a code. It had just to be translated. This would indicate that the message was not of special importance. Lossoshér, I'm afraid, you are going to be bitterly disappointed."

The Ferron was about to reply when the electronic brain spat out a white slip of paper. Rhodan seized the strip and read aloud the transcription of the message that had been engraved on the small pyramid of moon 13B.

"Many ways are leading to the light. Some are only detours. The trail points toward the right direction."

"What do you make of it?" asked Lossoshér.

Rhodan smiled. "It's meant to comfort those who have either lost the right track or never even found it. There are detours, on the path that will solve the Galactic Riddle. I believe, however, that the direct way is faster, even if it is more difficult. Thank you, Lossoshér, you have rendered me an invaluable service. And many thanks to you, Groll."

Groll left, his face a stoic mask, while Lossoshér had trouble hiding his disappointment.

After the door of the control centre had closed behind the two men, Khrest remarked, "I feel sorry for Lossoshér. He had hoped to bring you some valuable clue. Is his discovery of any real significance, Perry?"

"Yes, but only indirectly, Khrest. It's some diversionary manoeuver. Just imagine: a hollow moon, that could be an inhabited planet, that serves only the purpose to divert our attention from the right path! What king of people these must be to have hatched out such tasks for us to solve!"

"A race of mental giants, no doubt!" Khrest's voice expressed admiration and awe at the same time. "What a memorable occasion when we meet up with them.

I hope we will prove worthy."

"In case we do find them," Rhodan said in a serious tone, "then we *are* worthy, my friend."

"True. If we *do* find them! Sometimes I believe it would be wiser to give up our search. But there is more to our endeavour than merely finding the secret of immortality. If we can establish contact with a race of such superior intelligence, capable of laying a trail throughout thousands of years—beings that have become the masters of all dimensions—such a contact might save the crumbling empire of the Arkonides!"

"Or help the rising empire of Terra, Khrest!"

Khrest and Thora remained silent. They exchanged quick glances and left the control center.

Bell waited until the door had closed behind them. "You should not speak so frankly with them, Perry," he warned. "They still believe in the supremacy of their galactic realm. They have no idea that you plan to become heir to their fading empire. It would not be advisable to make them our enemies . . ."

"Khrest has no illusions about Arkon's future." Perry shook his head. "He fully realizes that his own race has become too weak to continue as the ruling force in the universe. He knows that mankind will become part of the heritage of the Arkonides. There is no doubt in his mind that this will be the best possible solution. He is on our side, Reg."

"You must be right, Perry, otherwise we would not be sitting here in the command center, in control of a spaceship that could return Khrest and Thora in no time to their own home planet. What are your plans now?"

Rhodan sighed. "Just wait and see what develops. We have no choice. We will never arrive at the solution to this galactic chain riddle if we overlook one of its links. And the underground vault in the Red Palace of Thorta was exactly that: one link in a long chain."

Bell left and Rhodan remained alone, sitting in front of the grand console of the computer brain. Fascinated, he observed the swift dance of the little bulbs that indicated the varying signals, listened to the inscrutable hum coming through the Arkonite metal of the hull. He could feel the vibrations of the positronic brain in action. Would the mechanical mind find the answer?

A long path stretched ahead of this intrepid astronaut, a path which, he intuited, would lead through not only space but time. Journey's end would be at eternity's threshold.

When the time came, would he have the courage to cross this threshold? For the destiny of mankind, he must not fail!